# The BOOB GIRLS

## The Burned Out Old Broads at Table 12

◈ ⟜ ❀⟐❀⟐❀⟐ ⟝ ◈

### A Novel by Joy Johnson

Copyright ©2009 Joy Johnson

ISBN: 978-1-56123-210-9

Library of Congress information on file.

GRIEF ILLUSTRATED PRESS

7230 Maple St.
Omaha, NE 68134

Order from: www.centering.org
1-866-218-0101 or 1-402-553-1200
centeringcorp@aol.com

# Dedication

*Dedicated to all my BOOB girl friends,
with special thanks to Louise, Carol, Mary, Maureen,
Jenny and Janet, Connie and her BOOB man, Dr. Mark Ware
and Brad Stetson.*

*A slow, easy thank you also to best-selling author, Robert Parker,
who sees everything, misses nothing
and has a handsome way of ambling.*

*And with all my heart's love to my own special BOOB man,
my husband Marv.*

# PART ONE:
# The Boob Girls

❖

*When a woman has three friends*

*Who will be there whenever she calls*

*That woman is rich indeed.*

# Maggie Patten

Maggie Patten was short, thin and just a little bow-legged. You could notice the legs right away because Maggie's dress of choice was almost always tight old jeans, flannel shirt worn outside her pants, dirty sneakers, all topped off with white, thin, minimum-maintenance hair. She had added one un-noticeable accessory to her already un-noticeable outfit. Today her flannel shirt hid an antique leather gun belt, complete with ancient holster and equally old Colt 45.

"Damn near perfect day," Maggie mumbled to herself as she pulled into the cemetery. "Damn near perfect." It wasn't yet spring, but one of those warm days that fools people into thinking they have a prayer that spring is just around the corner. The sky was gray, covered with a cold front moving in from the Nebraska plains. No clouds, just grayness that snuggled up against the tree tops and silenced even the birds perched in the big oaks that marched between the gravestones.

Maggie drove to a spot under one of the big trees and got out of her Jeep. The door slammed behind her. There was no need for stealth or silence. No one was around this time of morning, when the sun wasn't even willing to show itself behind the gray sky. She walked with purpose and deliberation, glad she didn't have Parkinson's or some other crippling monster that stole youth and bit your ass with unpleasant surprises. Maggie might be old, but she wasn't slow. She reached the grave she wanted in less than three minutes. She had dreamed of this moment for months, ever since she had put her long-suffering, self-serving, mean-talking husband in the ground. He had been sick only a few days and she had been his caregiver. Maggie Patten wasn't tired anymore. Maggie Patten didn't have anyone to wait on or change diapers for or lose sleep over except herself. And Maggie Patten had always been, if nothing else, a woman of purpose.

She took a stance taught her by her father when she'd been no bigger than a minute and their big old ranch in the Nebraska Sand Hills had been the only home she'd ever wanted. She stood strong and steady, pulled out the old Colt that had belonged to that same father and fired five shots into the Rock of Ages tombstone the marker company had finally set firmly at the head of her husband's grave. Shards of granite flew into the air.

"Never been anything but trouble, you sonovabitch," Maggie said to the grave.

She tuned, and without looking back, walked to her 1999 Jeep. A quiet drizzle began as she opened the door. The Jeep was her best, most loyal friend. It had not one rust spot, never drank too much oil and when Maggie had blown a tire on I-80 between Omaha and Lincoln one day, she had changed the tire in no time. It was like the old Jeep was actually helping her do it.

She unfastened the gun belt and gently laid it, the old Colt secure in the holster, on the floor in front of the passenger seat. Before she got out of the Jeep she would put it in a large carpet bag purse she'd thrown onto the back seat. Maggie figured the folks at Meadow Lakes Retirement Community probably didn't approve of guns.

# Mary Rose McGill

Mary Rose McGill didn't hear the shots from the old Colt fired by Maggie Patten, or if she heard them at all they were too faint to notice. Her hearing had been slowly going for years now but she was unwilling to go the hearing aide route. She struggled out of her old Chrysler Concorde and waddled up the hill toward the grave. Under her plain brown coat she wore a flowered print dress and a white sweater. On her feet were sensible shoes. The uglier they are, the more comfortable she believed and these were good with her almost constantly swollen ankles. She was sixty, okay, probably close to seventy, pounds overweight but she didn't care. She's tried every diet in the world and in the last five years or so, she'd let herself go. Her hair seemed to reflect her personality, mouse brown with a lot of dismal gray, dry with tight curls from years of home permanents. She would never have the pure thick white hair she envied in other women. Mary Rose knew she was boring and she had one boring arm hooked through the handle of an equally boring J.C. Penny shopping bag that held a $6.99 bouquet of flowers from the HyVee grocery and a simple, small stool. The blooms peeked out from the top of the bag.
Every week she made the cemetery trip to change the flowers in the metal vase on her husband's side of the marker that bore both their names. Only her death date was missing. You can put it in there anytime. *I'm ready,* Mary Rose thought. She was tired, tired of her clothes, tired of her car, tired of her life.

Mary Rose had four daughters, none of them close by. Her husband wanted a boy and being good Catholics, they'd never used birth control. Then when he'd decided he could only shoot girl seed, they'd just stopped having sex. Mary Rose didn't mind. Her husband didn't seem to mind, either. He went to mass every morning year round and she'd come to think of it as their "Holy Celibacy." It was during mass one morning when he had a massive stroke that blew his brain as thoroughly as Maggie's old Colt could have done. He had died just a few days later. At least he was where he had wanted to be, doing what he liked doing when it happened.

She took the dead flowers from the vase, tenderly arranged the new ones, and fixed the little stool next to the grave. She sat on it and spread the old flowers one at a time over the grass, reaching as far as she could without falling off the stool. Mary Rose had arthritis – some days worse than others and cemetery days always seemed to fall under "worse" - and she couldn't kneel and lay the flowers out for the life of her. Her mother had birthed eight children, never had glasses (Mary Rose had thick lenses in plain wire frames), didn't need a hearing aide and every joint in her body seemed to be equipped with its own personal tube of hinge oil. Mary Rose's mother had never liked Mary Rose. She thought her inferior, but then Mamma hadn't cared a whole lot for any of her children, especially the daughters.

"Not much going on here," she said to the headstone. "Want to know the truth, I'm lonely, lonely as can be, just plain lonesome." Her husband didn't answer. He had seldom done so when he was alive and things hadn't changed since he was dead.

There was a comfortable drizzle as Mary Rose limped back to the Concorde. It was a good old car and Danny at the gas station on the corner of her street had checked it every month when she had lived in her house. She would need to drive over and see Danny again soon. For now though, she headed back to the Meadow Lakes Retirement Community where there was neither meadow nor lake – just loneliness waiting for her.

## Hadley Joy Morris-Winfield

Hadley Joy hadn't heard the shots either. She was in the mausoleum in the east corner of the rambling cemetery putting a single rose beside the urn holding her husband's cremains. Hadley Joy was pretty sure it wasn't really him in the lovely jar. His plane had plowed into a mountain in Colorado killing him, the pilot who was his best friend and two other men headed to Aspen for a business retreat. The plane had blown and burned, and Hadley Joy believed the nice funeral director had gathered what he could of whatever was on the ground, put it in four body bags and shipped it back. She'd figured this out when the funeral director had discreetly asked for their names. She had the feeling with that question he didn't know how many were aboard. Didn't matter. It was the thought that counted.

She was a lovely lady and had the white hair Mary Rose envied. A friend had called it, "Vidal Sassoon hair" after the old television ad where the beautiful young woman had turned her head one way, and her hair flew slowly and gracefully in the other direction. Hadley was used to telling friends, "My hair and my legs are still great. Everything in between needs a little work." Not really. She could be called handsome. Nearly six feet tall, Hadley Joy Morris-Winfield,

the lady of four names and a hyphen, was graceful, trim –
though she had thickened a bit in the last few years - well
made-up and wearing a tasteful black pantsuit with a gray
turtleneck and gray boots. She had married well and it had
lasted. She liked big men and big dogs and her big man had
liked big cars and big cigars. They were comfortable together.

"I suspect our boy's anorexic wife wants to move into
the house," she told the urn. "He doesn't call. Talk to him,
will you? Tell him his old mother's going to write him out of
her will if he doesn't take her to dinner and fix her up with
some handsome old dude with tight buns and chest hair."
She leaned against the wall by the niche holding the urn and
talked on for nearly an hour.

The drizzle was a hopeful shower and Hadley Joy
snapped open her black umbrella as she walked back to
her white Land Rover. Her husband had driven a monster
Cadillac, she had a stylish Lincoln. The day after his funeral
she had driven the Lincoln to their friend who owned the
dealership and traded it in for the little Land Rover, used, or
"pre-owned" as they say now. The dealer had tried to talk her
out of it, but she was insistent. She'd always wanted a car like
this. It reminded her of the matchbox cars their son had loved
as a little boy. She turned the radio on to the classical station
as the rain came down harder and she headed toward her
spacious and exclusive top floor apartment at Meadow Lakes
Retirement Community.

# Robinson (Robbie) Leary

Robbie Leary did hear the shots Maggie fired into the big Rock of Ages stone. She stopped, listened for a full minute after the sound died away and tried to figure out what in the world the target had been. Kids shooting beer cans off a wall? She couldn't tell, but Robinson Leary knew gunfire when she heard it.

The grave she visited was in the new part of the cemetery where the markers were brass and laid flat in the ground. "A damned golf course for the dead," her husband had called it, but he was there now and he'd never owned a golf club in his life.

Robinson Leary, named after the famous black man who had base run the racial barrier out of the ball park, had skin the color of well-creamed coffee. "A perfect Latte," her sweet husband said once, holding her hand and pulling her down for a quick kiss. "If I don't get to walking and keep this weight off, I'll be a Grande," she'd smiled and they had gone down the elevator of their trendy Old Market apartment, down the ramp and onto 12th street, him letting her push his wheelchair so she'd build upper arms until they got to the river front walk where he would race her and almost always win.

They were professors together at the university. They were best friends. They were colleagues and companions and shared a big dining room table piled high with papers and books and journals with two laptop computers hidden away between the stacks. He had died in her arms, softly, unexpectedly, tenderly. They were spooned together in bed.

She had her knees tucked into the back of his, her chest against his back, an arm wrapped around him holding his hand when she noticed how cold it was. She had pulled the comforter tighter around him once during the night, but this cold was down-right scary. She had whispered his name, sat up in bed, rolled him over and knew he was dead. She had worried sometimes about long, painful deaths and while this had its own raw, unyielding pain she was relieved death had decided to be a silent night visitor.

She came to the grave once a month, on his death date. She brought their favorite flower, daisies, and sat crossed-legged on top of the cool brass marker that told everyone he hadn't lived long enough.

"I found a nice place with a goopy name," she said, "Meadow Lakes Retirement Community. Not far from campus or the Old Market. I got scared, Sweet Cheeks. Funny how we could be in the worst part of town after dark and walking beside your wheels, I'd never felt afraid, but without you – eight AM at Delice's Bakery gave me the willies." She sighed. "Time to go," she said. "I'll ride the long freight home to you someday, Baby."

Robbie Leary had taught English literature and loved it, but after her husband died the campus felt empty, her students seemed younger and dumber so she'd taken her retirement and moved out. Her Creole daddy had given her determination but not bravery and her half black, half-white mother had blessed her with practicality. Don't be scared when you don't have to be.

Robinson Leary was medium height, still reasonably trim with black-rimmed glasses that reflected her intelligence.

Her hair was straight and thick and fell just below her ears. She wore brown denim slacks and a matching jacket trimmed in suede. She moved with confidence and ease.

She enjoyed her talks with the spirit of the one man she'd loved in her life and she cried unashamedly as she walked in the gentle rain back to the old Volvo that had been their favorite joke. Intellectuals were required to drive Volvos. Everyone knew it. She headed the old Volvo away from campus, away from the rainy cemetery and headed toward Meadow Lakes Retirement Community, National Public Radio talking to her from the tinny speakers.

## No Politics, No Religion, But Sex is Okay

When Maggie, Mary Rose, Hadley Joy and Robbie returned to Meadow Lakes, there was a notice slipped under their doors. The plain white sheet of typing paper had words large enough for even the nearly-blind to see.

<u>DINING ROOM NOTICE</u>
<u>PLEASE RESPECT ALL DINERS</u>
<u>DO NOT TALK RELIGION OR POLITICS</u>
<u>BECAUSE OF RECENT COMPLAINTS</u>
<u>WE WILL ATTEMPT TO BUILD BETTER</u>
<u>COMMUNITY</u>
<u>BY ASSIGNING TABLES</u>
<u>YOUR DINING TABLE IS #12</u>

"Well don't that beat a dead horse," Maggie thought.

"Interesting," went through Hadley's mind.

"Oh my," Mary Rose said, shaking her head. "Something bad has happened."

Robbie held the paper up and read it aloud. "DAMN WELL SHOUTS AT YOU!" she said.

She was both curious and hungry when five o'clock came and the dining room opened. It was a pleasant place and the food wasn't half bad. Their monthly fee included, as her daddy used to say, "Three hots and cot," and most people took good advantage of it. Table 12 was in a corner by the full wall of windows and Robbie could see two other women pulling their chairs out to sit down. She walked slowly over to them. "Hi," she said. "I'm Robinson Leary. Call me Robbie." Twenty minutes later, the fourth diner arrived, huffing and puffing and disheveled. If she had been wearing a slip, Robbie thought, it would be hanging two inches down below the back of her dress.

"I'm late. I went to sleep. I'm Mary Rose McGill." Before she could even seat herself a Meadow Lakes server plopped a salad down in front of her.

Dinner was pleasant. They learned that the reason for the restriction on conversation came because of frequent arguments over the up-coming election, a loud discussion of gay rights in conservative churches and Maggie Patten's well-aimed dish of macaroni and cheese plastered over the bald head of a man seated next to her. Hadley Joy had laughed, Robbie had clapped her hands and Mary Rose's mouth had fallen open before she worked up a shy smile. "Just remember, girls," Maggie said as she finished the story. "No religion, no politics, but sex is okay." Maggie became somber. "I regretted it later," she added. "Mac and cheese is my favorite dish and I'd only had two bites."

Dinner was over. They had laughed and talked non-stop and now they lingered over coffee, the rest of the diners gone to their television sets or card games. There was a brief silence and Maggie looked at Robbie's dark skin. "I have a question for you," she said. A big smile crinkled her face and highlighted every wrinkle. "I always wondered, do black men have black balls?" There was total silence.

Robbie hesitated for just a beat. "Well," she said, "I don't know about all black men, but I do know about an old black man who was in the hospital with an oxygen mask over his face and this student nurse came in. He reached out toward her and said, "Nurse, nurse, will you check and see if my testicles are black?" She looked at him and said, 'Oh sir, I can't do that. I'm just a student nurse here to give you a sponge bath.' He looked really pitiful and said, 'Please! I've asked and asked and no one will check and see if my testicles are black.' Now she could see his heart rate was shooting up really fast and his blood pressure was going through the roof, so she said, 'Well, all right,' and she lifted up his sheet, took his manhood in one hand and his testicles in the other and said, 'No sir, they look perfectly normal to me.' As she covered him back up, he took off the oxygen mask, smiled at her and said, 'Thank you, that was wonderful. Now listen very carefully. *Are my test results back?*'"

There was just a second when all three women took a short breath. Maggie Patten slapped the table and hollered. Hadley Joy Morris-Winfield put both hands over her mouth and let tears roll out of her eyes. Mary Rose McGill, however, got up from her chair and rushed out of the dining room as fast as her stubby legs would carry her.

"Damn," Robbie said, "I think I offended her. I'm so sorry."

"Not your fault, girl," Maggie said, "I was the one who brought up the sex talk."

"You think one of us should go after her?" Hadley asked. "I don't even remember her last name…McGraw? McCall?"

"McGill" Robbie said softly. "Mary Rose McGill. A nice Catholic girl I bet. I am so, so sorry."

They sat for a few minutes in silence, and then they saw Mary Rose hurrying back to the table. "Sorry," she said as she sat down. "I started to laugh and I had to pee and I knew I was going to leak."

Robinson Leary walked slowly back to her apartment. It had been a long time since she had talked so openly, been so real. She liked these women, different as they were from one another. She whispered softly, "Now is the time, the walrus said, to talk of many things, of shoes and ships and sealing wax, of cabbages and kings." She knew every word of the old Lewis Carroll poem, and right now she felt a little like his Alice in Wonderland. She had walked through a mirror into a new world of older women, They hadn't talked of any of those things…shoes or ships or sealing wax, but they had talked of souls and sorrows and she knew Maggie Patten, Hadley Morris-Winfield and little Catholic girl Mary Rose McGill better than some of her friends from the university who had taught with her for years.

# What's A Nice Girl like You Doing in A Place Like This?

The next morning Hadley woke early, as usual and wrote in her journal. For years she had journaled and could never get the discipline to write consistently. Then she came on the idea of keeping the journal by the toilet. When she sat, she wrote. Somewhere in her storage bin below the big retirement complex years of journals lay in big boxes waiting to tell her everyday stories to any grandchild who would be interested. Hadley Joy sometimes wondered if any would be.

She poured a large travel mug of decaf coffee, read three chapters in her latest mystery book, checked in to see if Wolff Blitzer was still living at CNN – the man was there so much she was sure he had a cot in the back room – and just before the dining room opened she had settled into a warm bubble bath, book still in hand.

"I wish we had agreed to meet for breakfast," she said to her lavender-scented soap. Then it occurred to her that maybe the other three would be thinking the same thing. She finished her bath in record time, pulled on a new pair of jeans and a Nebraska Cornhusker sweatshirt, slid her feet into a pair of sneakers and did a slow jog down the hall to breakfast. The sun was shining in the window wall and for a second Hadley couldn't see if anyone was at table 12. Then her eyes adjusted and she saw three coffee cups raised to salute her. She broke into a grin and a power walk at the same time.

*What was it about honest conversation among women?* Robbie thought as she listened to the other voices at the table, talking fast, hands gesturing, laughter mixed with somber talk. "Giddy" was the word that came to her. Already they had agreed with Hadley about Wolff Blitzer having a cot at CNN and gone into a giggle-filled conversation about the tightness of buns on other newscasters. Mary Rose even entered in, and while not mentioning butts and thighs, said she really did deeply admire that African-American weatherman on the Today show.

"Al Roker," Hadley Joy added. "He's a hottie!"

It was Mary Rose who asked the obvious question, "Why are all of you here? At Meadow Lakes, I mean."

Robbie was straight-forward with an easy answer. "I wanted to be close downtown. I am purely and unashamedly addicted to people. And I am scared to be alone. A, B, C or all of the above."

Maggie had come from a ranch in the Sand Hills of Nebraska and had gotten, "as far away from there as I could get and I didn't want one of those new places in west Omaha. I refuse to live in a place where I'm older than the trees."

Hadley Joy had been more hesitant. "I loved my house and I had a beautiful garden, but after my husband died, I ended up just living in one room so when I got an invitation to the open house when this place first opened, I came and I signed. I figured that third floor apartment wouldn't last long." The server refilled their cups, three decafs, one regular. "What about you, Mary Rose?" Robbie said. "You asked the question.

"I didn't have a choice," Mary Rose said, looking into her coffee cup, her hands folded on her lap. "After the funeral, two of my daughters found this place, rented me an apartment and told me what they'd done when they started packing up my things. I should have known something was going on when a U-Haul parked out front, but that wasn't for me – it was for the stuff they were taking for themselves."

"They're poop-heads!" Maggie exclaimed.

"How could they do that?" Hadley asked.

"What did you do?" Robbie asked, reaching over and touching Mary Rose's shoulder.

"Moved in. What else was there? And it's okay. I got the furniture I wanted and now I'm coming to like it here."

"Still poop-heads," Maggie mumbled.

"Anybody want to come up to my place?" Hadley Joy asked. "I have some great movies."

## *Death Talk*

Days passed and the conversation at dining room table 12 at Meadow Lakes Retirement Community continued without mention of shoes or ships. Cabbages were never included, but after a movie afternoon watching Helen Mirren in The Queen, there was much discussion of the royal family and the death of the beautiful Princess Diana.

"She had no body fat," Maggie ventured.

"But she was so beautiful," Mary Rose added, "like a flower that had just come into full bloom then was plucked."

"I bet she was plucked more than once by that Dodi Fyed fella," Maggie said.

"In a way, she reminds me of my present daughter-in-law," Hadley said thoughtfully. "Frankly, I liked Elizabeth a lot better than Diana. And Phillip – what did you think of him?"

"Handsome, royal, gotta admire a guy who can be married to a ruler of the British Empire," Robbie said.

They were silent for a time, contemplating that daunting task that had aged the royal spouse into dignity and ownership of a white Stetson every time he visited Canada when the Calgary Stampede was going on.

Suddenly, out of the blue, Mary Rose asked one of her questions. "Your husband was dignified and royal-like I bet, Hadley. How did he die?" In this time of getting to know each other they had never talked about husbands or children.

"Airplane crash. Nosed straight into the Rocky Mountains," Hadley Joy answered soberly. She told them how she felt way down in her soul that those ashes in the urn were just remains not cremains. "How about you, Mary Rose?" she asked in return.

"Massive stroke while he was at morning mass," Mary Rose replied. "He lived for a few days and they were awful. The girls came and I just felt lucky that we had never hooked him up to machines because they would have fought over whether to keep him breathing artificially and eating through a tube. I wasn't ready to let him go but I wasn't ready to have him be a vegetable either. I worried about what would happen to me if we had to give all our money to a nursing home or rehab center. I don't feel guilty about it, you know, I just feel kind of bad that the thoughts went through my head and I looked over our insurance policies late one night when the girls were asleep to see how much I'd have when he died and what it might cost if he didn't."

"Grief and relief all wrapped up in the same package," Robbie said. Then she smiled a strange, magical smile. "What you did, Mary Rose was practical. I did the practical thing, too – and with some style I might add.

"My man died in his sleep - in my arms - and I'm nothing but glad it happened that way. My worry was that I didn't know whether or not I could get into our safety-deposit box after the death notice went out. I'd heard a couple of stories about having to wait on probate or some other legal crap, and I didn't want to take any chances. There was three months rent in cash in that box as well as our stocks and bonds and our funeral plans, so I covered him up, just like he was still sleeping and I was at the bank when it opened. It's that little bank with the heart logo so everybody knows us there, especially when you teach just up the street, live just down the street and come waltzing in a couple of times a month beside a wheelchair." She took a deep breath and a sip of her coffee.

"Anyway," she sighed, "I went up to the teller and said I needed to get into my safety-deposit box. Well, he smiled and said, 'You bet, Ms. Leary. Where's that professor husband of yours?' I didn't lie. I looked him in the eye and said, 'He's still in bed,' and I cleaned out that box, hurried home and called his doctor who didn't doubt for a minute that I had just woke up, called him right away and wasn't even dressed yet. Of course I was, but it didn't matter. He knew my husband had fought MS and infections for years, so I didn't have to go the 911 ambulance route – just the short route to the bank." She started to chuckle.

"He's still in bed! You are SO SMART!" Mary Rose exclaimed.

Hadley Joy and Maggie joined in the laughter and no one noticed that Maggie Patten hadn't said a word about how her husband died.

# A Little Poker Music

The "no religion no politics" rule at Meadow Lakes died its own ignominious death as well it should. People went back to old friendships or switched tables depending on who was in the dining room at any given meal. But the occupants of table 12 never changed. There was laughter, tears and serious conversation three times a day.

They were almost always together. There were afternoon movies at Hadley's apartment, trips to the Old Market for brunch or lunch or just strolling around the historic area. They joined the bus trip to the zoo and walked the botanical gardens as the weather warmed up. Sometimes while Maggie sat at a table, drank coffee and read the newspaper at their favorite brunch spot on Sunday mornings, the other three went to a new church on the river walk and hurried to meet her afterward. Saints Mark and Matthew church, known affectionately as "Saint M&M's" was lively and fun and combined a good dose of New Age thinking with old time evangelism that was refreshing. "It never hurts to know God loves you," Robbie had said.

They spoke of grief and what it can do to you, mentally, spiritually, emotionally and physically. They visited the cemetery together now, with Maggie visiting the other graves but never her husband's. When the death anniversary for Robbie's husband rolled around they all took flowers to his grave, held Robbie and cried with her.

Maggie admitted outright that she wasn't all that bent out of shape when her "sonovabitch" died. Robbie knew she would always have a hole in her heart, as would Hadley Joy, and one day Mary Rose confessed that she didn't think she was "doing this grief thing right," because she was happier than she'd been when she was married and in her own house.

One day at dinner Maggie pointed to a table a short distance from table 12. "See that old dude in the brown vest?" she asked. The other three looked and nodded. "I heard early on that he does his laundry every 15th of the month at midnight and sits in the laundry room butt naked. That way he can do all this dirty clothes at once, even what's on his bent old back."

"No!" Mary Rose exclaimed.

"Really!" Hadley responded.

"Who would have thought it?" Robbie asked.

"Want to go see?" Maggie asked and crinkled her whole face into a smile. "Tonight's the 15th."

There was silence then Mary Rose said, "I'll have to take a short nap first. I'm never up that late."

## *Wiley Vondra*

At midnight sharp they met in front of Mary Rose's apartment. It was closest to the laundry room around a corner and down the hall. Mary Rose uttered a soft giggle as she opened the door and slipped out. The soft lighting was as secretive as their mission and they tip-toed down the hall even though the other residents were either fast asleep, trying to get fast asleep or dozing in front of their televisions. Just in case, Maggie took the lead, motioned them to stop at the corner and peered around to make sure the coast was clear. She motioned them on and stopped at the closed laundry room door so fast that Mary Rose bumped into her. "Shhh," they both said together. There was soft country music coming from inside. Another cowboy had lost his woman, his pickup and his dog to the cruel fates of life.

"Here goes nothing," Maggie said and she threw open the door.

Sitting at a card table was Wilson (Wiley) Vondra. He had a hand of solitaire spread in front of him and was wearing a battered old Stetson hat, wire-rimmed glasses, the brown vest, brown leather cowboy boots and nothing else. For just a second his gray eyes registered a mild surprise. Then he smiled a smile that rivaled Maggie's and in a voice surprisingly deep said, "Evening ladies. Want a nice hand of poker? There's a stack of chairs in that closet."

"Oh, I couldn't," Hadley Joy said, blushing slightly.

"I wouldn't," Robbie said, staring unabashedly at Wiley.

"I shouldn't either," Mary Rose whispered.

"I'll get the chairs," Maggie said.

The music came from a small CD player at Wiley's feet. Willie Nelson was on the road again and Mary Rose was the only one who had no idea what poker really was or how to play it. Wiley was good at explaining and they agreed to play two practice hands so everyone could get the feel of it.

Mary Rose was a quick study, and never once mentioned that all card games were prohibited by her growing-up home and church. When she had practiced successfully she took off her glasses and polished them on her white sweater. "This isn't going to be one of those strip poker games is it?" she asked.

Wiley smiled. "If it is, little lady, you'd better put those specks back on. They'll probably be the first thing you want to take off." Hadley Joy reached up and touched her ear. She was glad she hadn't taken off her earrings.

## Beauty is...as Beauty is

Table 12 sat empty and expectant the next morning at breakfast. Wiley Vondra sauntered in, looking clean and pressed, and sat down with three other men at table #15, just three places away from the lonely table by the window wall. He was the only one who glanced at table 12.

At lunchtime, however, table 12 was fully occupied and surrounded by the sound of eager whispers. As things quieted down, Mary Rose leaned even further in and said in a conspiratorial voice, "I want to lose 50 pounds." The others looked at her and waited, "Since we've been at this table, "she continued, "I've lost 10 pounds and I need to lose 50 more, Maggie, you're skinny as a rail. Robbie, you're just right and so are you, Hadley. You look like I'd love to look – thick white hair, tall and graceful and your posture is great. Makes you look even taller than you are."

Hadley smiled, "I'll tell you the posture secret, "she said. "A couple of years ago I was with my 13-year-old granddaughter and all of a sudden she said, 'Gram, if you don't stop walking with your head down all the time I'm going to be taller than you are.'"

"I was doing what old people do, walking stooped over, leaning forward, looking down to see where I was going. So I got a book on stretching that had a section on posture. It had this formula: Shoulders back, Head high, Eyes straight ahead. Tummy tucked in. So I made it into an acronym and changed "Eyes" to just the letter "I" and told my granddaughter to say it out loud to me every time she saw me walking like an old lady." She smiled and leaned back in her chair.

Robbie began to smile back. "Cool acronym," she said.

Mary Rose struggled with it. Maggie remained silent.

"First letter of each word….." Mary Rose mumbled. Shoulders, Head, I, Tummy

SHIT!" she said loud enough for the diners next to them to turn and look.

"I love it!" Mary Rose said, and clapped her hands.

## The Remake

"We all need to do some work on ourselves," Robbie said, "We could walk every day."

"Wait a minute," Mary Rose held up her hand. "There's more. I want a new hair-do and I want to get some makeup."

'This isn't about Wiley, is it?" Hadley asked, her eyes opening wide.

"No – it's about me," Mary Rose said. "And I need some new clothes. Do you know what's in my closet? Nothing! I spent the morning bagging up all my clothes and throwing them down the garbage chute."

They stared at her.

"Fourteen lousy housedresses! That's what I had, Fourteen! No slacks or jeans just crappy old lady housedresses." Her cheeks were getting pink. "And look at these shoes! First rate stupid. Let's go shopping! Right now!"

"Where is she now? Robbie asked Hadley.

"Last seen in jewelry."

"Where's Maggie?"

"Last seen in auto parts."

They both looked at their watches. The trip to the Target store was lasting longer than they had anticipated. Mary Rose had already had a make-over in cosmetics and  shoes, socks and hosiery had found their way into her shopping cart as she went through department after department. On her trip through underwear, Maggie had thrown a red thong into her cart when she wasn't looking.

Maggie scurried toward them, breathing hard. "She's finally in the dressing room doing the pants and shirts thing. This is getting boring. Hurry up. Follow me."

"She said that all in one breath," Robbie said. They followed.

Maggie led them to a miserable rack of ugly prom dresses marked 70 % off. "These are every degree of ugly," Robbie said.

Maggie smiled a wicked little smile. "Yeah."

When Mary Rose finally emerged from the dressing room, her arms full of clothes, she dropped her bundle and her mouth fell open.

Maggie was posed like a model in an off-the-shoulder mint green extravaganza, her boney shoulder blades making her look like a parakeet in drag. Robbie struck a Sophia Lauren pose in a skin-tight black dress that emphasized her love handles and Hadley sat in a chair, one friend on either side, her legs demurely crossed and wearing a horrendous blue job with puffed sleeves and even more gigantic puffed bottom.

# Peyton Claireborne

Mary Rose hurried, dressed in a jogging suit and led the other three women in their first one-mile walk around the Meadow Lakes complex that ended at table 12 in time for dinner.

"I'm going to be sore tomorrow," Mary Rose said. As soon as dinner was over she excused herself and said she wanted to try the new hair color she had bought at Target. "I've never done this," she said, "but it looks easy. No help on this, girls. I want to surprise you in the morning."

Morning came, but Mary Rose was nowhere in sight. She wasn't at table 12 when the others arrived. She wasn't there when they had their second cup of coffee. She wasn't there when they went through the breakfast buffet and started eating.

"Think we should call her?" Robbie asked.

Just as Hadley opened her mouth to answer, her cell phone rang.

"It's her," she said. She listened and her face darkened. "She's crying and she says it's an emergency."

They stood together and rushed out of the dining room, "Mary Rose?" Robbie said as they knocked on her door. "It's us, honey."

The door opened and Mary Rose stood in front of them, still in her bathrobe.

"Christ in a cracker jar! I'm surprised all right." Maggie exclaimed.

"Oh Mary Rose! Sweet Mary Rose!" Robbie wailed. Hadley Joy pulled out her cell phone and hit speed dial. "This is a Peyton Claireborne emergency," she said.

Mary Rose's hair was in spikes and the color of an orange clown's wig.

They drove Hadley's Land Rover, Mary Rose sitting quietly in the front seat with one of Hadley's expensive silk scarves over her head. Hadley pulled up in front of a huge warehouse in the Old Market district and led them to an elevator.

The Old Market was an historical delight, brick streets, wooden awnings reaching over the sidewalks with colorful petunias hanging down from the tops of the awnings. Trendy restaurants were in every block, horse-drawn carriages took tourists on slow, romantic rides and street musicians entertained on shaded corners.

"I've been all over the Old Market," Robbie said as the elevator stopped, "and I never knew there was anything other than condos in this building."

"Exclusive and somewhat secret," Hadley replied.

On the top floor, with huge ancient windows that overlooked the Missouri River, was a salon and spa so modern it could have fit into any Fifth Avenue venue in New York City. The door opened with a tasteful chime and immediately they were met by a towering, thin black man whose hair was cropped and dyed a brilliant pink. He wore a purple t-shirt with "Queen for More than A Day" embroidered in rainbow colors. The belt of his tight black jeans held an assortment of his tools, combs, scissors, small implements and other things known only to Peyton Claireborne. His feet were comfortable in black sandals that showed off his red painted toenails. He kissed Hadley in both cheeks and she hugged him hard.

"Thank you for seeing us, Peyton," she said,

and turning to her friends added, "Girls, this is Peyton Claireborne, the best stylist in Omaha and one of my surrogate sons."

Peyton nodded an acknowledgement and scurried toward Maggie. "Oh my dear," he said, reaching down, placing one hand on her shoulder and picking up a strand of thin hair with the other. "It is indeed an emergency, but nothing Peyton can't fix."

Maggie's mouth flew open, she jumped and took a step backward.

"No dear," Hadley said, touching Peyton's arm. "This is our victim," and she pulled the scarf off Mary Rose's head. Peyton studied the disaster.

"I rather like the color, but on you, Darling, it's definitely not a photo shoot. Come with Peyton, sweet thing, and we'll fix you up." He looked at the three others standing by the door and gave them a delicate Princess Di wave. "Out you go, sweethearts. Peyton needs privacy for this one." Ninety minutes and six cups of coffee later Hadley's cell phone rang at their table at Delice's Old Market Bakery.

"She's done," Hadley said.

"So he's gay as three hummingbirds, but who the hell is he?" Maggie asked on their walk back to the salon.

"The most beautiful drag queen in Omaha," Hadley answered. "You wouldn't believe his legs."

"He thought my hair needed help," Maggie complained.

"It does," Hadley and Robbie said together.

Peyton sash-hayed over to them when the little chime rang as they walked in. "May I present," he said, gesturing toward the curtain by his styling station, "The Lady Mary Rose!"

The curtain was pulled back and all three women gasped. Mary Rose had what was almost a burr cut – close and cropped and framing her face with what appeared to be bangs all the way around.

"Holy Moly. Knocks my socks off!' Maggie said softly.

"Wow," was all Robbie could say.

"Peyton, you have worked a miracle," Hadley Joy said. The color, a soft, pale blonde, fit Mary Rose's complexion and gave her an entirely new personality. Her face was made up and radiant. In her hand she held a small designer bag with the salon logo on it.

"And Peyton gave me a make-over," she said, holding up the bag. "No more of that cheap crap, I'm going with the real stuff here. Maggie, you can have the Target make up." Maggie turned, opened the door and walked out.

"I'll take the Target stuff," Robbie said.

Mary Rose and Hadley stayed behind for a minute to hug the master stylist and Robbie shook his hand.

## Sick and Sicker

They walked every day. When the weather was bad they hit the state-of-the-art workout room at Meadow Lakes. The only other person ever in the room was a buff elderly gentleman who never spoke to them or looked their way and acted as if he deserved to have the equipment all to himself.

"Good buns though," Robbie remarked.

"Lots of hair," Mary Rose added.

"Pecker the size of a cocktail weenie," Maggie judged.

At least twice a week they met at Hadley's apartment

for Afternoon Movies, skipping lunch so they could eat microwave popcorn and drink diet sodas. On three occasions Wiley joined them, bringing Westerns that Maggie applauded and the others relished. *Appaloosa, Unforgiven*, and *3:10 to Yuma* rated two-thumbs up from all five reviewers and Robbie convinced Wiley they were really chick-flicks in disguise.

"Sweetheart," he argued, "they are westerns, man stuff, guy movies. Chick flicks are soupy love stories with dogs in 'em."

"Wrong, tough guy," Robbie had responded. "Any movie with Ed Harris or Clint Eastwood or Russell Crowe and Christian Bale are chick flicks."

"Or Brian Dennehy or Bruce Willis," Hadley added.

"And big old Brian baby was in the best western ever, *Silverado.*"

"I'll give you that one," Wiley admitted. "I'm not buying Bruce Willis, though."

I'd buy Johnny Depp," Mary Rose said.

It was on a non-movie afternoon that their walk took them through the cemetery. Visits to graves had become a part of their walk. The cemetery was huge and on their cemetery days they could wind through the quiet, pleasant paved paths and get in more than three miles. On this day they came over a gentle hill into view of a burial tent and a small crowd gathered beneath it, but it was the group standing at a distance from the mourners that attracted their attention."

"They have signs," Mary Rose said. "I can't make them out." Hadley and Robbie took several steps closer and bent forward as if that would help them see better.

"Too far away," Robbie said.

"I know who they are," Maggie said, her voice almost

a growl. "The one sign says God Hates Fags. The other sign will have the name of that poor soul they're lowering into the ground and will say, So-and-so Rots in Hell. There will be a couple more saying God hates America because of queers or something like that."

It was quiet as everyone looked at Maggie. Tears were rolling down her cheeks. "I don't want to talk about it now," she squeaked and began walking toward the crowd beneath the burial tent. The others joined her, standing just outside the tent in silent support. As the service ended, they saw Robbie hurrying down the little hill, carrying the small bouquet of flowers she had left on her husband's grave.

"He would want him to have these," she said, and tenderly handed them to Maggie who, after the mourners began to file out from under the tent, moved forward and placed them on the casket beside a spray of roses with a banner than read, "Beloved Son."

No one asked Maggie about the tears that day, and they might never have except for one unfortunate event. A new strain of flu virus ripped through Meadow Lakes Retirement Community with the speed and destruction of a northern plans tornado, flattening people into their beds and emptying the dining room.

Coughing filled the hall ways. Robbie was the first to show symptoms.

She dropped into her chair one morning, hair uncombed and her face damp with sweat. "I should have called," she said, "but I felt pretty good when I got up. I'll pass on walking."

No sooner had the words left her mouth than Hadley Joy bent over in a coughing fit. Maggie pushed a glass of water into her hand, but it didn't help.

"Shit!" Hadley said, "And I don't mean the straighten-your-shoulders-and-tuck-in-your-tummy word. This is crappy." Her voice was already becoming hoarse. She stood up. "Come on, Robbie. You might as well get your pjs on and come to my place. We're in for the day."

"Do you get dizzy with this?" Mary Rose asked.

"You're always dizzy," Maggie answered.

"Well, I guess I'm joining you then," Mary Rose said, leaning on the table as she stood up.

"Wimps," Maggie said. "I'm walkin.'"

Mary Rose, Hadley and Robbie were in their bathrobes wrapped in Hadley's afghans and lap blankets, tissues in hand, glasses of water with lemon slices by their sides half an hour into the first Harry Potter movie when Hadley's doorbell rang. Standing in the hall was Maggie, in bathrobe and slippers, a small cloth comfee tube tucked under her arm. She held it up for Hadley to see. "Heat it in the microwave and put it where it hurts," she said. Then looking past Hadley to Mary Rose and Robbie, in the most pitiful voice they had ever heard she whispered, "I threw up."

It was during the second film of their Harry Potter Marathon movie watching that Maggie announced she was going to lay down on Hadley's bed for a "little quick shut-eye." At 9pm the third movie ended and Hadley saw Robbie sound asleep in one of her two small recliners. Mary Rose was snoring softly on her couch. Hadley walked quietly to her large bedroom closet, took out two blankets and covered each woman lovingly. Then she went to her bedroom, turned down the covers and crawled in next to Maggie, snuggling into the queen-sized bed on the side that had once belonged to her husband.

The next morning they were better but still weak. They had taken turns at Hadley's shower until it ran out of hot water. They were make-up free and even Robbie looked pale. Still in their bathrobes, they gathered at Hadley's table. Maggie grabbed a slice of dry toast, buttered it and complained about having only decaf coffee.

Mary Rose reached over and rubbed Maggie's back. "What were those tears about in the cemetery, Maggie?" she asked, "When we saw those people with signs."

"They were sicker than we are," Robbie said.

Maggie leaned back in her chair and took a bite of toast.

"We've never talked about our children," she began. "Oh, we know about your four poop-head daughters, Mary Rose, but only that they stuck you in here. We don't even know their names." She looked at Hadley and Robbie. "Nothing about kids from you two yet," she paused, then went on.

"All of you know about the Sand Hills. They're beautiful and exotic. There's actually sand there." She smiled. "I remember looking at Chimney Rock, the landmark for the wagon trains and actually seeing the ruts their wheels made. There's no more beautiful sunrise than over those Sand Hills. I grew up out there in a small town and I married a small town guy – businessman. Successful. Heavy drinker. Hard hitter. A real bastard, but I loved our place and I loved the town. We had one boy. His name was Harley.

"The long and short of it is after high school he went to California to college. He was our only child and I was hoping he'd at least stay close, but California called to him. He was good about keeping in touch though. He had a good job out there and then when he was thirty years old he came back for a weekend and surprised us. That afternoon I went out for some groceries and when I got back, Harley and his dad were gone."

"A couple of hours later his dad came back and I asked him where Harley was."

"Gone for good and I hope dead," he said and he went to the closet where we kept our rifle. He looked at the gun and said, "Nope. Not dead, the little shithead."

Robbie's eyes widened. "I don't get it."

Mary Rose gasped. "What did he mean, not dead?"

Hadley leaned forward.

"Our boy had come back to tell us he was gay," Maggie said, her voice hardening. "He'd waited to tell his dad first because he didn't want him and me to get into a fight over it – and we would have – I'd have stood up for my boy.

"My husband was a bastard in a lot of ways and if you look it up in the dictionary "bastard" is someone who doesn't have any real relationships. That sonovabitch had said to Harley, 'Son, I'm going to go walk the fence line. There's a rifle in that closet. You know what to do with it.'"

"You know what to do with it?" Mary Rose asked. "What did he mean?"

"He hadn't said it outright, but what he meant was for Harley to take the rifle and kill himself." She paused and Hadley poured her more coffee.

"I never saw Harley again. When I called his apartment a young man answered and said Harley was dead to us. I yelled, 'Not to me! Not to me! Tell him I love him!' But I never heard from him again. I went to California and tried to find him. When the television news showed all those gay couples getting married I recorded every newscast and looked for him in the crowds. I searched the internet and got pretty damned good at it, too, but I never found a trace. And that's why I could kill those other bastards who hold hate signs."

They were all quiet.

"My girls are Mary Claire, Mary Elizabeth, Mary Ruth and Mary Louise," Mary Rose said softly.

"All Marys?" Maggie asked, her eyebrows lifting.

"What can I say?" Mary Rose asked. "We're Catholic," and she added more coffee to her cup. Hadley walked to the sink and started another pot.

"They're okay," Mary Rose said. "But when I called and told them I'd lost weight and had a new hair style and new clothes and really enjoyed it here, I thought they'd be happy. They weren't."

"Mary Claire said, 'How could you do that to Daddy?' Well – what did I do? Was I supposed to stay dowdy in memory of him?" Mary Rose blew her nose into a paper napkin.

"Mary Elizabeth said, 'It's about time for Pete's sake.' And the youngest, Mary Ruth told me she wasn't helping me pay for any new clothes. I hadn't asked her to pay for any. I didn't even call Mary Louise. I just gave up."

"Poop-heads," Maggie said.

Robbie looked up from her cup. "I had three children," she said.

They waited.

"Had?" Maggie said.

"Had. One was a miscarriage. I don't know what the sex was. One was a little girl who was stillborn and the other was a sweet boy who lived for two weeks. Then I had a hysterectomy and that was that. I mothered the kids I taught at the university."

"I have a son," Hadley said. "He's a good man whom I never see. I wrote in my journal one day, 'there is a loved stranger living in my heart.' He's a lawyer and a good one I guess. He's on his third marriage to a mean woman who practices Olympic thin. She is a stick! I've never mentioned eating disorder – I don't see her enough to talk to her. My favorite daughter-in-law was the first one. They had three children – all of them are in college now and I still keep in touch with her and the kids. She's an artist in Sioux City. As for the other two wives, poop-head would apply," she said and patted Maggie's head as she reached for the fresh pot of coffee. Robbie looked at them and smiled. "There was a black woman writer," she said, "an older lady who wrote about dancing on your newly-waxed floor and the warmth of a good bath. One thing she wrote I always remembered, even after I forgot her name. She said something like, 'It's amazing how one continues to watch for signs of improvement in one's middle aged children.'"

"It's sad when your children don't care if you're alive or dead," Mary Rose said.

"Sadder still when they wait for you to die," Hadley added.
They nodded.

"It's noon," Mary Rose said. "I feel better. I'm hungry." Together they walked to the dining room, still wearing their bathrobes. The big room was nearly empty from flu victims. They ate all their lunches then went back to Hadley's to finish the Harry Potter marathon. Everyone but Hadley had missed most of movie number three.

The next day the manager of Meadow Lakes brought up the subject of a dress code for the dining room at the weekly staff meeting.

# BOOB Girls

It was three more days before they got back to the routine of meeting at table 12 and walking. The first morning back Mary Rose hurried to the table. "I found something important," she announced excitedly.

They waited.

She posed sideways.

"What!?" Maggie asked.

"A waistline!" Mary Rose squealed. "I have a waistline again."

Her shirt was tucked in and sure enough – she had a waistline.

Their walk, however, was not exciting. They were still tired from being sick and as they turned into Meadow Lakes, Mary Rose was rubbing her hands together and Robbie was breathing hard.

"We need tea," Hadley announced and they followed her once again to her apartment on the third floor.

"Growing old sucks, like they say," Robbie said.

"I have this stupid arthritis," Mary Rose complained. "It hasn't bothered me for a long time but if I get a little weak, it acts up. I remember my mother saying the man Arthur Ritis only visited weak women, so I guess he moved in with me after the flu."

"What else do you have, Mary Rose," Hadley asked. "If

it's just arthritis you're lucky."

"Oh the usual, I guess, blind as a bat without my glasses, enlarged thyroid, deaf in one ear.

"Sexy people are often hard of hearing," Robbie smiled.

"What did you say?" Hadley laughed and they high-fived each other as they gathered again at the table.

"Actually," Mary Rose said. "I really am lucky. You said you had a hysterectomy, Robbie. Was that because of the babies?"

"Fibroids that thought they were queens of my body," she said. "No, my big health deal is a little heart thing."

"There is no such thing as a little heart thing, my dear," Hadley said.

"Well, it could be worse," Robbie continued. "I have an atrial flutter. My heart spins out of control and shoots up to around 200 beats a minute. I have to go in and have what's called a cardioversion – an electric shock to the heart. I told my cardiologist one time that if she wanted me to have a shock to my heart she could have a bunch of old men run by me naked. She said the problem was finding old men who could run. I keep it pretty well controlled with meds. If it starts to pound I take a couple of pills and it usually quiets down."

"I had a hysterectomy too," Hadley joined in. "Cancer just four years ago and it was a really good experience for me. It took awhile for me to be able to say that, but it was." She chuckled.

"My OB-GYN was young and cute as a bug. He did a biopsy and when he pulled the biopsy tube out it looked really good and he said, 'Fantastic,'" I said, "Do you know what it means to a lady my age to have a handsome young man look between her legs and say, 'Fantastic!'" She had folded her hands demurely over her heart.

"Jesus!" Maggie said. "That's good."

"Your turn, Maggie girl," Hadley said.

"Not much here," Maggie replied. "I have macular degeneration – you know, you hear about it all the time. The most common cause of blindness in persons over 60. I'll eventually lose my reading vision, but hell, I don't read much anyway. Had a bleeding ulcer, but he died." She smiled. "And I'm borderline diabetic and ugly as sin. That does it for me."

"Peyton awaits you," Mary Rose said.

"We've been sick, we've had heart trouble and cancer and we're going blind, bleeding inside, have goiters and are stiff as rails. We're a bunch of burned out old broads." Robbie reported with a smile.

Mary Rose thought for a minute. "Burned Out Old Broads," she said. "We're the BOOB girls."

They were getting to know each other, as few friends ever do.

# Thelma and Louise

The four friends had a comfortable, pleasant, enjoyable routine. They ate together, walked together, watched movies, and went to the theater, the art fair and the museum. Once they went to the symphony where Maggie snored through the second half. Hadley, Mary Rose and Robbie went together to get styled by Peyton Claireborne while Maggie sharpened her straight-edge razor and cut her own hair. They watched as Mary Rose lost three pounds and gained two back, lost four pounds and gained two again. On occasion Mary Rose took an afternoon off to write letters or read, Hadley met friends outside Meadow Lakes for coffee and Robbie got together with teaching colleagues from the university.

While three of the four grieved their losses, talking about it with each other, sharing memories and making cemetery visits helped. Indeed, comfortable, pleasant and enjoyable pretty well described their lives until one movie afternoon when it was Maggie's turn to choose the movie. She dug through Hadley's movie cabinet to pull out the old 1991 hit, *Thelma and Louise*.

They were silent as they watched Susan Sarandon and Geena Davis fly off the cliff in their old convertible.

"What a break-away movie," Hadley said, "the first adventure, buddy, road movie with two female leads."

"Break away for Susan Sarandon for sure," Robbie added. "It catapulted her right into my movie radar."

"Catapulted that '66 Thunderbird straight into a scrap heap," Maggie added.

Mary Rose sniffed. "I've always dreamed of doing

something like that," she said. "Taking off and leaving no forwarding address. I just love those words, *no forwarding address.*"

Hadley Joy Morris-Winfield nodded and smiled. "So have I. When things would get stressful or worrisome for me, I'd imagine how I could just disappear – go to some little town in Canada –and no one would find me. I'd put my mind to how I could get money, a different car, a new identity and that would give me some distance from my troubles and when I came back from the day dreams I could think clearer." She paused. "Not that I'd ever really do it," she said softly.
No one said anything,

"We could do it," Maggie said. "We could leave with no forwarding address. If you think about it, things have gotten a little boring around here."

"But if we left and were gone months on end wouldn't we miss our children?" Mary Rose said.

"So?" Hadley said.

Mary Rose looked at her for a moment. "I'm in! But how do we do it? Where would we go?"

"Give me a minute," Maggie said. "I need to make a phone call," and she pulled out her cell phone and went into the bedroom for privacy.

"It could be fun," Robbie said.

"It could be exciting," Hadley added.

"It could be an adventure!" Mary Rose exclaimed.

Robbie stood and spread her arms, "'We were schooner-rigged and rakish, with a long and lissome hull, and we flew the pretty colors of the cross-bones and the skull, we'd fly a big black Jolly Roger flapping grimly at the fore, and we sailed the Spanish Water in the happy days of yore.' John Masfield, 1913," she said and did a small bow.

"We could even take a cruise," Mary Rose said.

Maggie came in from the bedroom and looked at Hadley. "Got a legal pad?" She asked. "And maybe we should have another pot of coffee. This may take awhile."

## Extortion Most Sweet

They sat at the table, the legal pad positioned in front of Maggie. A pen was poised over it, "OK, what do we need and what do we have to do to leave here and have some fun?"

"To go adventuring," Mary Rose corrected.

"We need money," Robbie said, and Maggie, in large letters, began to write out a list.

Money – enough for six months or more.

"If we think about six months," Robbie said, "we'll need to have enough to pay our rent here for that length of time. Do all of you have direct payment from your banks?"

They nodded.

"But I'm not sure I'd have enough to pay rent and take enough with me," Mary Rose said, "I spent a lot on clothes and Peyton."

Hadley thought for a minute. "Let me get the traveling money," she said, "and when we come back, you can pay me back."

"We don't want anybody to know where we are," Maggie said. "Mary Rose, your four girls will want to get you back under control. Somebody from the University will be asking about you, Robbie, and Hadley sooner or later that son of yours is going to realize his future endowment has flown the coop."

"Right. It's not an adventure if we just treat it like a vacation," Mary Rose said.

"Just one new cell phone," Maggie said. "We need a cell, but they may be smart enough to trace our calls."

"They can do that?" Mary Rose asked.

"I don't know, but they can on television shows."

"I want the cell phone where that cute little nerdy guy has all the people following him around," Mary Rose said.

"The network."

"My laptop should be untraceable if I don't go into email," Robbie said.

"Here's the deal," Maggie said. "Awhile back I had a call from Millicent, a niece I don't much like – my brother's girl. She said I need to go up to the Sand Hills and talk to my brother, Homer. He's dying and no one is telling him. I'm the one to tell him and he has the wheels we need, ones big enough for us and our stuff and it will be cheap living. I'll hide my car with him." She looked at each of them. "We each take one small suitcase, that's all."

"It will be more of a mystery if we just take one car and they find the other cars here," Mary Rose said.

"It will be more of a mystery if they never miss us," Hadley added. "When do we go?"

"Tomorrow's good for me," Maggie said.

"I need to visit Peyton," Mary Rose said.

"I need to visit Peyton," Robbie said.

"I need to visit Peyton," Hadley added. "And I'm going to need three days to get some cash – I assume we're taking cash not using ATM's all across the country. But after the Sand Hills, where do we go?"

"'We go, my lovelies, my instant loves – where we are led by stars above.' Student paper, last year," Robbie shrugged. Mary Rose blushed. "It's the fifteenth in three days. We could say goodbye to Wiley. He's good at keeping secrets." They looked at her. Maggie did a quick eye roll.

Hadley thought for a minute. "Okay," she said. "I know how to do this. Robbie, do you have Photoshop or anything like that on your computer? Maggie, you said you got good on the computer when you looked for Harley. Can you doctor a photo?" They both shook their heads.

"Wiley has all kinds of photo stuff on his laptop," Mary Rose said.

"How do you know that?" Robbie asked.

"I need to go down to my storage bin and dig out some pictures," Hadley said. "Mary Rose, see if Wiley can meet us at his place right after dinner."

Wiley had five shots of whiskey on his table along with his laptop computer when they got to his apartment. Maggie grabbed hers and downed it. Mary Rose did the same. Robbie and Hadley watched her then looked at each other, eyebrows raised. Hadley sipped her shot and Robbie pushed hers toward Wiley, "Heart problem," she said. Wiley drank both.

"Here's what we need, Wiley," Hadley said and she stood behind him and showed him what she wanted done with a small stack of different photographs.

"Bit tricky, but no prob," Wiley said. "You girls want more whiskey, it's on the counter over there."

Maggie was the only taker.

Not one BOOB girl slept well that night.

Maggie thought about a rustic log cabin somewhere in Alaska where mountains towered over it and winter snows covered half the cabin. Hadley saw herself in the sunny southwest, living in an adobe house and wearing long, colorful skirts. Robbie pictured a glass-enclosed home looking out on one of the Great Lakes with a boathouse and beautiful sailing ship docked near the back deck, and Mary Rose dreamt of lying on the warm beaches of California and for the first time in her life, getting a sun tan. Unfortunately, none of these dreams would come true.

## *Johnny Wray Winthrop the Third*

Early the next morning Hadley Joy Morris-Winfield, dressed in moderate heels and a business suit walked into the expensive and expansive office of her stock broker, Johnny Wray Winthrop III carrying a briefcase. She greeted Megan, his receptionist and asked about her children. "They're just fine, Mrs. M. Growing like little weeds," and she ushered Hadley into Johnny Wray's private suite with its stunning view of the city.

"Hadley Joy!" Johnny Wray said and gave her a warm hug. "What can I do for you?"

"It's simple, Johnny Wray," I want $250,000 cash, day after tomorrow. Sell whatever you think best."

Johnny Wray looked stunned. He didn't speak for awhile, then he said, "I can't do that, Hadley. Everything is tied up and with the market where it is, you don't want to sell."

"Yes, dear, I do. And I need it day after tomorrow."

"Hadley, have you talked to David about this? He wouldn't want his mother to do anything foolish."

"Frankly, Johnny Wray, I haven't talked to him and you are not to tell him. I know you've been best friends since grade school, why, you're one of my surrogate sons. I love you like my own, but this is totally, absolutely personal and private."

"What do you want to do with all this money?"

"I'd like to tell you it was a surprise for David and his family, but I know you'd ask him if he'd gotten it yet, or if he knew what it was, and while it is a surprise for him, he won't know anything about it for some time." She leaned back in her chair and gracefully crossed her long legs. Johnny Wray glanced at her legs then quickly looked away.

"I'm not sure I can do this, Hadley. I'm not willing to lose my friendship with David over it. He and I are a lot more than golfing buddies and besides, his name is on most of your securities since his dad died. A lot of that would require his signature. In addition, your time frame is almost impossible to meet."

"Oh, you can do it, Johnny Wray. You have networks and connections and I've heard you talk about deals you've made, $250,000 afternoon of the fifteenth."

"That's a quarter of a million dollars!"

"Your math is excellent, Johnny."

He continued to shake his head, looking just a little smug and patronizing. Hadley waited. Finally she reached down and picked up her briefcase.

"I had really hoped it wouldn't come to this, Johnny Wray. Our families go back a long time. But I have something to show you that I think will insure that I not only get the cash – remember that's cash- but that you'll also keep this professionally confidential." She reached into the side pocket of her briefcase and pulled out a manila envelope containing two photos.

"Remember that nice benefit party we had at our place when my skinny-freak daughter-in-law got involved in the children's charity?" She asked. "You'll be interested in these pictures of you and her in my bedroom."

Johnny Wray took the pictures and stared at them. "These aren't real! I was never with your daughter-in-law in your bedroom and for certain sure I never had my hand on her butt or looked at her that way! Well maybe I looked but not like that! She's in a bikini for Pete's sake." He looked again, "Geez, I didn't think she was *that* thin!" He was beginning to bluster. Hadley pressed on.

"Now I know they're fake, and you know that, darling. But your sweet wife, Rebecca doesn't know that and neither does my trusting son. I would definitely not approve if this caused him to leave Ms. Skinny and go after wife number four. To tell you the truth, I'd at first thought about talking to Jim, the manager at Happy Hollow Country Club where you spend so many afternoons and see so many clients. As you know, Jim and I go way back and I could just mention a few improprieties toward me and I imagine your tee times would become very difficult to arrange and your business table by the windows over the 14th green would find itself unusually occupied, but that really wasn't strong enough." She re-crossed her legs and rested her elbows on them, placing her chin gracefully in her hand. "To do both unless I absolutely have to seems a bit overkill to me, don't you agree?"

"Hadley Joy, this is blackmail!"

"Actually, dear, it's extortion - I'm getting money through force, intimidation and compelling argument. I looked it up. I'll be back here, day after tomorrow, at two o'clock. I have a hair appointment at one. I suggest you leave the money in one of those suitcases with wheels at the front desk with Megan. That way if push comes to shove you can at least say you didn't see me take it."

Johnny Wray nodded and looked at his nervous hands. Beads of sweat were forming on his forehead.

Mrs. Morris-Winfield smiled and said goodbye to Megan, went into the hall and pushed the elevator button. "I've always wanted to do something like that," she whispered to herself as she stepped into the elevator. She smiled all the way to the lobby.

## *Free at Last, Free at Last*

They were so excited they could hardly stand it. Realizing all of them were likely to have second thoughts, they had made a pact. Maggie had put her hand square in the middle of table 12 the morning after they had decided to make a run for it.

"No backing out!" she said with some force.

Hadley Joy had slapped her hand on top of Maggie's, "No losing nerve."

"No broken promises," Robbie said when she slapped her hand on top of Hadley's.

"And no chicken excuses to quit!" Mary Rose said, completing the stack of three pale hands and one dark one.

It was time to leave as soon as they said goodbye to Wiley. They all tried to nap the afternoon of the 15th. Robbie ended up going through her poetry books for the fifth time to see which three she could fit in the one allotted suitcase. Hadley had taken a walk alone, selected eight of her favorite movies to slip between her clothes, pulled a book from the stack by her bed, but was unable to read herself to sleep Mary Rose sorted her clothes for a fourth time. Maggie slipped out to the corner QuickStop and bought a pack of cigarettes. She hadn't smoked since before her husband died. She sat outside the little convenience store, chain-smoked three cigarettes then stood, threw the pack away and walked back to Meadow Lakes.

They talked softly during dinner that evening. Maggie told them they would get to her brother's ranch late in the afternoon and then she'd show them her idea for going on. She wanted to keep it a secret, she told them, because you never know how things are going to turn out, and if this didn't work she didn't want a lot of questions, they'd just play it by ear and go on from there after she'd told Homer he was dying. "It's kind of like, 'good news, bad news,'" she'd told them. Her brother was several years older than Maggie. Having been sick for years, he was 'weak as a newborn piglet,' "I can say it like this," she rehearsed, "Homer, the good news is – you're dying. The bad news is – you're dying," For some reason it didn't come out as humorous as she'd planned, and the other girls just nodded knowingly.

At last the witching hour rolled around, the minute hands on their watches seemingly stuck and unmoving toward midnight. Johnny Wray had come through, and Hadley Joy rolled two small-sized suitcases into the elevator, looking both ways to make sure the hall was clear, even though there were only three apartments on the entire third floor. The elevator stopped at the second floor and Robbie and her suitcase got in without them saying a word. Robbie carried a small stuffed black bear under her arm and for some reason it gave Hadley a degree of comfort.

Maggie came out of her room on the first floor as they approached. She'd had the door open a crack watching for them. Mary Rose opened her door without their knocking and they went together to the laundry room and Wiley Vondra, pulling their suitcases behind them.

Wiley was naked as ever, his boney white arms a sharp contrast to the brown vest he always wore. "Ladies, ladies, ladies," he sighed. "I do wish I could go with you. Never know when you'll need a good man around," and he winked.

"Thanks for everything, Wiley," she said. "We didn't want to leave without saying goodbye." She hugged him and he pulled her head back and gave her a kiss on the mouth that was just a few seconds longer than a peck." Maggie rolled her eyes and Hadley and Robbie looked at each other.

"Bye, Wiley," Robbie said and gave him a quick hug that didn't touch more than the vest.

"Take care, Wiley," Hadley said and held out her hand. Wiley took it and put it to his lips.

"Wiley," Maggie said as she nodded at him, "thanks for the shots, ya old dude."

Wiley, clothes and modesty free, insisted on helping them load their luggage into Maggie's jeep. He lifted his hat in a salute, turned and walked bare-assed back into Meadow

Lakes. They stood quiet for a moment, and then Robbie spoke. 'Did you know," she said, "that according to Marie Sandoz, our great Nebraska writer, cowboys on the plains only had one pair of jeans they wore every day. And since they were always in the saddle, those jeans wore clear through. The men would walk down the streets of the early towns without seats in their trousers, butts just a bare as Wiley's."

"Maybe he represents a true and sacred piece of history," Mary Rose said, and she actually sighed.

Maggie looked into the night sky. "Look at that full moon, a good sign, leaving with a full moon over us."

"Have you ever howled at the moon like a wolf?" Robbie asked. "A couple of my friends went to Montana with a group who did just that. They howled at the moon and the wolves howled back."

They looked at the moon then at each other, "Owww-wwwwwwwwww! Yip! Yip! Yip. Owwwwwwwwwwwwww!" They howled together. On the third howl, a light came on in Meadow Lakes' second floor, followed by a second light, and the four wolves dived into the old jeep and crept out through the gate, heading into the strong, persistent Northern Plains wind blowing enthusiastically out of western Nebraska.

They stopped for an early breakfast in Lincoln, at an all-night restaurant with an old gas station motif. Light from ceiling lamps reflected on antique pumps and gave a cozy glow. It had been exciting to pull into the truck stop and park by the slumbering eighteen-wheelers. The clean, crisp air felt good, and even though not one BOOB girl had slept well, they felt refreshed and most of all, they felt: "Young," Robbie said, "I feel Young."

"And excited."

"And hopeful."

"And hungry."

They ordered omelets and pancakes and bacon and eggs and all the things they had gone without while they worked on becoming fit.

## Homer Millet

Maggie's brother owned a huge spread deep in the Sand Hills. The old Victorian house stood sentinel over the plains and was unlike the neat Queen Anne's and other Victorians in the cities and small towns of Nebraska. This was a big ugly monster with one gigantic turret, peeling paint and a chimney that had long ago collapsed.

"How many rooms does that thing have?" Robbie asked, peering out her window.

"Twenty four," Maggie answered. "He lives in three of them."

Ancient fir trees surrounded the house and served as a wind break to the prairie winds. Behind the house a big barn that had seen better days was silhouetted in the late afternoon sun.

Maggie ignored the driveway that formed a circle in front of the house and headed the jeep over the bumpy lawn to the back. A once-beautiful porch circled three-fourths of the house.

"He lives back here," she said. "I'm gonna take you girls into the back parlor and go talk to Homer. He'll be in the kitchen. If I want you to meet him, I'll give a holler, but it may be best he not know you're even with me."

Hadley wondered how anyone could not know they were with her. The porch steps creaked and groaned and when she put her weight on the top step she was sure she heard something break beneath her.

Maggie led them into a spacious, dusty Victorian parlor and said she would be back in a little while. "Make yourselves comfortable. I'll yell if I want you to come meet him."

"Didn't this used to belong to the Munster family?" Robbie asked, and she quoted Mary Hewitt's old poem, "Will you walk into my parlor? Said the spider to the fly, Tis the prettiest little parlor that you ever did spy. The way into my parlor is up a winding stair, and I have many curious things to show when you are there." They jumped as two clocks began to strike simultaneously, one a grandfather clock that reached nearly to the 12-foot high ceiling. "Curious is right," Hadley said.

"Five O'clock," Mary Rose said. Dust motes floated in the sunlight coming through the large, dirty windows. Hadley went to one of the antique settees in the room, patted it and sat down after the dust settled. Robbie took a straight back chair near the grandfather clock. Three more clocks in the parlor were wound and working. Tick, tick, tick.
Mary Rose went to the door behind which Maggie had disappeared. "I can hear them talking," she whispered. "I can't make out much. I heard him say, 'bastard'."

"Talking about her husband," Robbie whispered.

"He says he got what he deserved and she did the right thing and I think she said he did too, but it might have been something about 'screw.' Can't hear.... can't hear…she says she's talked to somebody……he called her a name, sounded mad…can't hear."

Several minutes passed. Voices from the kitchen were too low to be heard. The clocks ticked on and struck the half-hour.

"They're nice clocks," Hadley said,

"I think I heard one in another room strike, too." Robbie said.

The next thing they heard was Mary Rose screaming. "Snake!" she yelled, "Snake!" She was jumping backward, pointing to one of the old floor vents. Coming out of it was the biggest snake any of them had ever seen. A massive head was followed by at least four feet of body and the tail was no where in sight. It looked at the women with sharp, beady little eyes, its tongue flicking faster and faster.

"Oh my God!" Hadley yelled.

"Sweet Jesus!" Robbie cried.

"Holy Mother of God!" Mary Rose yelped and together they dived and stumbled through the door to the kitchen.

"Hello Ladies," Homer said. "I see you've met Methuselah."

Homer Millet was a very small man. Sitting beside him on an old porch glider, brought inside years ago, Maggie looked absolutely massive. He was wrapped in a patchwork quilt, his feet disappeared into soft house slippers designed like cowboy boots and could not have looked more ridiculous if they'd been yellow duckies. A winter cap was pulled down over his head and he had mittens on his hands.

"Homer," Maggie said, "I want you to meet my friends, the BOOB girls."

"I'd stand ladies, but it means I'd have to take an extra nap to perk up again. But feel welcome. I'm sorry about my friend in there. He's a giant bull snake and he patrols the house and barn and keeps out the rats and prairie dogs. Went through three of my housekeepers in one month and there's not a wild chicken who'll come near the place." He fell into a laughing fit that ended in a serious coughing spell. Maggie patted him on the back while Robbie, Hadley and Mary Rose looked on wild-eyed.

"He ate the housekeepers?" Mary Rose said in a shocked voice.

"No, no – not at all," Homer answered. "They just quit. He tends to like to be around people and they weren't necessarily snake people. One I have now is fine though, Mexican girl, used to 'em in her village back home. Feeds him eggs every time she goes to the grocery. Lets him curl up by her when we sit here and watch the TV."

Hadley thought Mary Rose might faint.

"Since you've met both my men," Maggie said, smiling. "We might as well stay the night. Homer, call the Mexican girl and tell her she can have the rest of the night off. Better if we leave early in the morning anyway."

Homer picked up the phone on the glider beside him and dialed a number.

"She's bossy," Mary Rose whispered.

"Demanding," Hadley said.

"Definitely in charge here," Robbie replied.

Maggie went to the refrigerator, scoured the cupboard and pulled out the ingredients for dinner. Country pork chops and packaged potatoes along with home-canned green beans and sauerkraut turned out really well and Robbie ate the extra pork chop, "Home cookin'." She sighed happily.

After the dishes were washed and put away Maggie said, "Come sit, everybody. You girls might as well help me with this," and she gathered the kitchen chairs in a semi-circle in front of Homer, who had eaten dinner on the glider and had not moved since they'd arrived. Maggie sat next to her brother.

"Ho-Ho," she said, calling him by his childhood name. "Millicent called me. She said the doctors had talked to her but they were afraid to talk to you. We have some hard news, Ho-Ho." She paused, took one hand out of its mitten and held it. "You're gonna die," she said softly. "The docs say it won't be much more than three, maybe four months, but you're gonna die and what I want to say, Homer, is you need to get right with the Lord and right with your family. If you do that, if you die - - it's okay, and if you don't - - that's okay, too. You'll always know I love you. There. That's what I come to say." There was a long silence. Hadley noticed at least two clocks were ticking in the kitchen where they sat. They all looked at Homer. All at once he broke into a crinkled smile almost identical to Maggie's.

"Maggot, good old Maggot," he said. "I know that! For heaven's sake does that girl of mine think I don't? Do you think I don't? I've been waitin' for death to come have a beer with me for over a year now," he patted Maggie's hand and Robbie saw tears glisten in her eyes. "I don't want you worryin' about me, Maggot, and I don't want you comin' back for me when I die. I'm so old nobody in town knows me any more so there's not gonna be a funeral. I'm gonna be cremated in the hot fire and dumped."

He smiled again and took a deep, rasping breath. "I don't know where you ladies are headed," he said, scanning all their faces. "I've put some things together from listenin' to you while you ate. You get on your trip tomorrow. Take what you need from the barn, sister. Mad Millicent Millet, daughter to the gods, won't miss it – I paid for it anyway and will leave it to you in my will." He bent over into another coughingfit. "And you'll like this, Maggot – I left the house and the land to Chipita, the Mexican girl. Millicent will have a fit but it's iron clad, by God, and there'll always be a home here for Methuselah." The clocks throughout the house struck nine.

They gathered their suitcases and drug them up creaking stairs to a large room with two twin beds and one double. "I had these made up in case something like this happened," Maggie said. I'll be staying downstairs with Homer. Get up when you want and we'll have breakfast and be on our way."

"I have one question, Maggie," Mary Rose said. "Where does Methuselah sleep.

"Between Homer and me on the glider of course. Night all."

"I'm stiff from riding all day and sitting so long tonight," Mary Rose said. "We should practice our SHIT." And they all straightened their shoulders, held their heads high and tucked in their tummies.

"Ho-Ho and Maggot," Robbie said. "What do you think she'd do if we called her that?"

"Hit us," Mary Rose said.

"Kill us," Hadley said.

They got ready for bed and crawled in. "I'm not going to sleep a wink," Mary Rose said.

"I know I won't either," Hadley said.

"Same here," Robbie added.

By the time the thirty clocks throughout the old house struck ten, all three women were sound asleep.

They woke to the smell of coffee and bacon. Breakfast was tasty and filling and snake-free. After they had eaten, Maggie said, "When you bring your suitcases down, bring your bedding, too – pillows as well. We'll probably need 'em." Robbie looked at Hadley and shrugged. Twenty minutes later they were saying goodbye to Homer. Maggie hugged him long and hard and kissed his cheek where Robbie could see tears running down the creases.

Outside the jeep was nowhere in sight. "In the barn," Maggie said.

They followed her to the big old barn, pulling their suitcases over the bumpy ground, holding their sheets, pillows and bedspreads tight against their chests. The sun was up and the day was clear and crisp. They could hear meadow larks in the distance and cardinals calling from the fir trees.

Maggie dug into her pocket for car keys. "We have new wheels," she announced.

She struggled for a second with the latch on the barn door, then threw it open.

Mary Rose gasped. "That is big," she said.

"That is massive," Robbie said.

"That is a frigging behemoth!" Hadley added.

"That's a Hummer," Maggie said, and she tossed the keys from one hand to another.

"And behind door number two," she exclaimed and opened the second half of the barn door, "is our home away from home."

Parked securely in the barn was a thirty four-foot light weight aluminum travel trailer with two slideouts.

"I've never gone camping," Mary Rose said.

"I used to," Robbie said.

"I considered roughing it a hotel with no cable," Hadley said.

"We don't have to take it," Maggie told them. She smiled her crinkly smile, but it had freedom and no forwarding address written all over it."

"Hitch the sucker up!" Hadley said. Mary Rose nodded.

"'Today is bright with promises, motivated by dreams, swept clean by winds of change and challenged by new themes,'" Robbie recited. "Clark Couch," she said with a smile, "genuine cowboy and poet. Let's get on with our promises and dreams and find out what theme is waiting for us out there."

Maggie backed the big black Hummer H2 out of the barn, turned it around and positioned the hitch directly under the hitch cap of the trailer on the first try. She hopped out of the truck, pulled stabilizer bars out of a side door of the trailer, fastened them securely with a minimum of banging and clanking and turned, wiping her hands on a towel. "Load 'em up, move 'em out!" She yelled.

The women threw their suitcases and bedding into the trailer and climbed into the Hummer. Hadley stayed behind to close the barn doors. As she pulled the second door toward her she saw Methuselah, coiled up, looking big as a truck tire, in the spot where the trailer had been. He was looking straight at her, his tongue flicking in and out.

# PART TWO:
# No Forwarding Address

*Like a band of gypsies we go down the highway*
*We're the best of friends*
*Insisting that the world be turnin' our way*
*And our way*
*Is on the road again*

Willie Nelson, **On the Road Again**

---

*Complications arose.*
*Ensued.*
*And were overcome.*

Captain Jack Sparrow

# Happy Campers.

Maggie drove the Hummer and tag-along trailer down the road to a large parking lot where a long-deserted restaurant sat wind-blown and lonely on one end. A sign that had once said, "Grandma's Home Cooking" hung down in front of the door. The windows were boarded up and grass was growing between cracks in the parking lot.

"Everybody drives," Maggie announced. "We each drive for fifty miles then switch seats all the way around." She got out of the Hummer. The others followed.

"We won't get bored that way," Hadley said.

"Our butts won't get flat," Robbie added.

"We won't get those terrible blood clots in our legs and die," Mary Rose concluded.

Maggie rolled her eyes and tossed the keys to Mary Rose. "You first, sweetheart. I'll ride shotgun."

Mary Rose pulled herself into the driver's seat. Hadley looked at Robbie, "It may be more dangerous to stay out here," and they climbed in the back seat.

Mary Rose put the keys in the ignition and the engine growled. She shifted gears, stepped on the gas and the big vehicle leaped forward, "Oh my!" Mary Rose said. She began to creep down the parking lot.

"Death at five miles an hour," Robbie said to Hadley and Mary Rose stepped on the gas, throwing them back against their seats.

"Step on the brake!" Maggie yelled. Mary Rose did and they all fell forward, the heavy trailer clanking to a stop behind them. Hadley and Robbie reached for their seatbelts.

"I can do this," Mary Rose said under her breath. "I can do this," and she slowly drove around the parking lot, letting out frightened little squeaks between, "I can do this." She circled the lot twice and Maggie gave her two thumbs up. "Now we learn to back up," she said. Robbie and Hadley unfastened their seatbelts and jumped out.

"No sense being part of a train wreck," Hadley said. Robbie nodded.

They took turns with Maggie serving as driving coach. Robbie recited poems of courage as she circled the lot and then backed up. Hadley announced that she really didn't need this as she had driven Cadillacs and Lincolns and knew about big cars. Maggie glared at her. Robbie and Mary Rose glared as well.

When Hadley hit the empty garbage bin at the back of the restaurant it left only the smallest scratch on the Hummer. "I can fix that," Hadley promised. "Get in," she added. "I get the first fifty miles." She pulled out of the parking lot and an eighteen wheeler swerved around her, its air horn blasting.

They were on the road only minutes when Robbie, riding in front with Hadley exclaimed, "This thing has satellite radio!" Together Hadley, Robbie and Mary Rose said. "We can get Wolff Blitzer!" Maggie did an eye roll.

"And a hands-free phone." Mary Rose said.

"It's paid up for two years." Maggie said. "Emergency calls only."

They stopped early their first day out, finding a small campground just over the border in Wyoming. There were a few trees and now and then tumbleweed blew through their site. Maggie taught them all how to hook up the electrical and sewer connections and put blocks in front of the trailer tires. They hadn't yet been inside the trailer and they were interested. Maggie opened the door first, pressed a switch and the couch and dining table slid out. "Stay here," she said. She hopped inside, went to the sleeping area, pressed another switch and closets slid out as well.

"Pretty smooth," Robbie said.

Inside, the trailer was divided into four sections. One to their left held two bunk beds and a half bath. A fairly spacious living area with efficiency kitchen lined one wall opposite a sizeable couch, dining table and four chairs. Two reclining chairs were tastefully arranged with a small table between them. A bathroom with glass shower was next and led into a bedroom with the slideout closets and a queen-sized bed.

"It's like playing house," Mary Rose said.

Maggie and Mary Rose drove into the little town near-by while Hadley and Robbie put away clothes, made the beds with the bedding brought from Homer's and explored the neat, well-equipped kitchen. Robbie played with the wide screen TV while Hadley ran through channels on the radio.

When Maggie and Mary Rose returned, they unloaded basic groceries and Maggie pulled out a chilled bottle of champagne, opened it and poured four glasses, "To us – the Boob girls," she said.

# Edith Ann

After only a few days the four women had worked out a routine. They rotated beds weekly so everyone had a bunk to herself while two others shared the queen-sized. They worked out a schedule for the shower, whoever wanted to clean and vacuum did so and they took turns cooking. Hadley had always wanted to try gourmet dishes and they found recipes she needed online with Robbie's laptop and enjoyed exotic dishes that alternated with Maggie burgers, Mary Rose's goulash and Robbie's family Cajun recipes. The days were extremely pleasant. When they became bored they moved on. It was in a campground further into Wyoming when, early one morning, Maggie jumped out of bed and threw open the door.

"What?" Robbie asked.

"Gunshots," Maggie said, "three of 'em."

There was silence.

"You sure?" Robbie asked.

"I'm sure."

The rest of the day was quiet, but that night, while sitting outside in their newly-purchased lawn chairs, Hadley was sure she had seen bright little eyes reflected in the car lights that passed their trailer as another camper returned home. For just a minute, she thought of Methuselah.

No gunfire interrupted them in the following two days. On the third morning Hadley had laundry duty, and as she worked in the little campground laundry room folding clothes she kept hearing a soft rustling sound. She opened the door to the adjoining bathroom and investigated. Nothing.

She kept folding and listening and just as she was about to leave, heard a weak mewling sound.

She listened, her head turned toward a large garbage bin. Slowly she walked over to it, opened the top and looked down on a small, obviously sick Schnauzer. The little dog growled, backed as far away as it was able to do in the cramped garbage can, and looked at Hadley with terrified eyes. She didn't hesitate a minute. She grabbed one of their towels, reached down, quickly wrapped it around the little dog and lifted it out of the garbage.

"Oh sweet thing," she said tenderly, "poor sweet thing."

The little female was almost skeletal, her ribs showing even through her fuzzy coat. Her eyes were runny and Hadley saw scars around all four ankles. There were open sores on her back.

Leaving the laundry, Hadley hurried back to the trailer with her sad little bundle.

The three others put down their books and stood up when they saw Hadley nearly running toward them. They gathered around in a tight circle as she drew back a corner of the towel. Huge frightened eyes looked up at them and they could all see the little dog was trembling.

"Oh my," Mary Rose said.

"Oh dear," Robbie said.

"It's a damn dog," Maggie said.

Hadley told them about finding her in the laundry garbage.

"Poor, poor little thing," Mary Rose said.

"She's nearly starved," Robbie said.

"No dogs in the trailer."

"Look at her little furry face."

"Look at her sweet little nose."

"Look at the scars on her little feet."

"No dogs in the trailer."

Robbie and Mary Rose rubbed the little dog's stomach and stroked her head. The trembling stopped and a tiny tongue reached out and licked Robbie's hand.

"No dogs in the trailer," Maggie said again.

The three surrounding the blanket raised their heads in one movement and glared at Maggie.

"No dogs," she said again, her voice growing weaker. There was a very long, eerie silence. The breeze stirred the trees and birds twittered. From somewhere else in the campground a dog barked once.

"Shit!" Maggie said and walked away.

The other three straightened their shoulders and tucked in their tummies, but their heads stayed bent over the tiny bundle in Hadley's arms.

"She looks like she's never been bathed," Robbie said as they climbed the steps into the trailer.

"I have a whole bottle of Peyton's shampoo," Mary Rose said.

They filled the kitchen sink with comfortable, cool water and Hadley gently lowered the little dog into it. She trembled just a little but was too weak to protest very much. As they rinsed off Peyton Claireborne's thirty dollar designer shampoo, Robbie bent down and looked at the dog's cheek where a dark mass was melting into the water. "That's blood!" she said. "And look at this, girls, this isn't a scratch. She's been shot in the cheek. That's from a bullet."

They held the little head up and stared.

"The shots Maggie heard - they were shooting at her," Hadley said.

"We didn't hear anything last night," Mary Rose said,

"I bet they shot her while we were at the bookstore late yesterday afternoon," Robbie added, "or we just didn't hear it during the night. They probably dumped her in the laundry because they empty that garbage every noon. They thought she was dead."

"She nearly is," Hadley said. "She needs a vet. Look at those sores." Small clumps of fur had loosened and floated in the dirty water.

It took three separate washings to get the little dog clean.

"I wonder what she feels like," Mary Rose said as she dried the tiny body, "being clean and all."

Robbie took an egg from the refrigerator, broke it, smashed the shell into small fragments and mixed it with just a little raw hamburger. She sat the bowl on the floor and Mary Rose sat the dog down beside it. The little dog sniffed once, bent her head into the bowl and ate the egg and meat in two bites.

"Hungry." Robbie said.

"Ya think?" Hadley said.

"I'll take her to the doctor," Robbie said. "There's a vet on the way into town. We drove past the office when we found the bookstore."

"No you won't," Hadley said. "We're in Wyoming, girl. You're the only black person we've seen and they'll think you did this to her. Mary Rose and I'll go. You take care of the pout we're getting."

"Where is Maggie?" Mary Rose asked.

"Sitting outside in her lawn chair where she can hear everything we're doing," Robbie said.

Mary Rose leaned over the sink and looked out the window. "Is she smoking?" she whispered.

## George Foreman, DVM

Hadley wrapped the dog in a dry towel and she and Mary Rose headed the Hummer into town. The vet's office was a small one, dealing more with cattle than pets. The sign on the door read, "George Foreman, DVM."

"George Forman?" Mary Rose said.

Hadley shrugged and opened the door. A bell attached to the door clanged and a round, pleasant-looking man walked out of an office. "Can I help you ladies?"

"We're just passing though," Hadley said. "And we found this little dog. She's been bathed but she's in really bad shape." She handed the veterinarian the bundle.

George Forman, who looked nothing like the former boxer, led them into an examining room, unwrapped the towel and stroked the dog from head to rear.

"Puppy mill," he said. "Hate those bastards. Wonder how this one survived. They breed 'em out, like this one here, then turn 'em loose in the hills for coyote bait. Where'd you find her?"

Hadley told him and they watched as Dr. Forman did an exam. "She's probably five years old – and that's a long life in a puppy mill. Some places license them as 'dog farmers' if you can believe it. See these scars on her legs?" he carefully held up one tiny paw. "They stack these dogs in cages, sometimes five cages in a stack. When they're little like she is, their feet go through the cages and get cut. I've seen dogs that have lost a foot through infection or chewing it off to get out. It's brutal."

The little dog appeared to doze under his hands. He treated her sores, gave her shots and pushed a vitamin down her throat.

"Some of these sores are probably from excrement build-up," the doctor said. "The poop and pee from the dogs in the top cages runs down on the dogs below. Maybe once a day, maybe less, the mill owner will take a hose and spray the dogs from the top down, washing the excrement from top to bottom. If that's not bad enough, they feed them what's been swept up from the dog food factory floors." He signed. "Kinda represents the evil in the world, don't it."

He tucked the little dog under his arm and led them out of the examining room into the main office. "Since you're not gonna be here long," he said, "I'll not ask you to fill out any forms. And you don't owe me anything. You take care of this old girl and this one's on me." He opened a door and gave Mary Rose a handful of ointment tubes. "For her sores," he smiled. "She's a lucky, lucky girl. Enjoy her."

When Mary Rose and Hadley returned, Robbie and Maggie had the clothes from laundry folded and put away. They were in the lawn chairs, reading and drinking coffee. Mary Rose sat the little dog on the campsite picnic table. She was wearing a bright red collar and every few minutes shook her head trying to shake it off.

Hadley laid out their purchases, dog food, a brand recommended by the vet, the ointment, dog toys and treats. Maggie didn't say anything, but she smiled a small smile and shook her head ever so slightly. Hadley told them about the puppy mill.

"So what we gonna call her?" Maggie asked. She led them inside and brewed a fresh pot of coffee. There were two coffee pots now on the kitchen counter, purchased on their first shopping trip, one for regular, one for decaf.

They sat at the dining table with the little dog snuggled into Robbie's lap and dozing. She had eaten one small can of dog food while the coffee brewed and they could see her stomach swollen with the unexpected bounty of food.

"We could call her Scroungy," Robbie suggested. "She is that."

"Or Lady," Mary Rose suggested.

They went over name after name. None really fit.

"How about Edith Ann?" Hadley asked. "Remember Lily Tomlin in *Laugh In*?"

"Edith Ann," Mary Rose said.

"Edith Ann," Robbie repeated.

"Hey, Edith Ann," Maggie said loudly. "You wanna be the fifth Boob Girl?"

Edith Ann jerked awake, looked around and barked one sharp little bark. Then she scrambled out of Robbie's arms, jumped down and peed on the floor.

# The Ragged Ass Saloon

They left early the next morning, before dog shooters and other vermin were out and about. Riding along, singing with the 50's station on the satellite radio was fun and Hadley Joy thought how this was one of the most interesting times of her life. She looked over at Maggie, sound asleep on the back seat beside her, Edith Ann curled up on her lap, making little movements with her paws as she dreamt.

Around three o'clock they came across a pleasant, wooded campground beside a big lake that invited them to "swim, hike, boat and bed down." They readied the trailer and took a short walk with Edith Ann. Even after only a day, she was obviously brighter, eating voraciously and loving all four women equally. She didn't bark or whine, she simply joined in the group and did her part by just being there.

"No cooking tonight," Robbie suggested. "Let's find a fun restaurant."

"It's early," Hadley said, "but so what. I'm hungry right now."

They drove about five miles and came to a small town. The sign coming onto Main Street said, "Welcome to Resolution." Robbie began to laugh.

"Oh, man," she said, "*Resolution.* Remember *Appaloosa?* The western? Well the sequel to that was a book called, *Resolution* by Robert Parker. My husband had a Parker collection of every book he wrote. Wow. I wish we'd known there was a real *Resolution* before he died." She leaned out her window to get a better look at the town. "If they had a dirt street and wooden sidewalks, this could be the old *Resolution.*"

Main Street stretched long and quaint. The streets

were brick, attractive and a little uneven. Wooden awnings shaded every business. Newly-planted flower boxes filled with petunias hung on the ends of the awnings and beside the support poles were old beer kegs planted with begonias. There were the usual stores, a grocery, a little post office, a bank in what looked to be the oldest of the buildings, a drug store, a library nestled in a city offices building, an outfitter, boat rentals, a wilderness guide, a few antique shops, a hardware and clothing stores. Two churches, across the street from each other along with a sizeable garage and filling station were at the end of Main Street. For all practical purposes, it could have been built, and probably was, at the turn of the century between 1880 and 1900. "No café," Maggie said. She was driving. They had spotted a bowling alley featuring food, but after one look they all shook their heads.

They drove around the town, which had about a ten-block area of old homes, some truly beautiful Victorians. Just off Main was a prize example of a Victorian Queen Ann, or "painted lady" done in various colors of that era. Other homes were tasteful prairie cottages with big porches and huge yards. There apparently had been no new construction for years. "Must live off the lake," Maggie said, and they headed south on a county road.

Barely half a mile down the road they spotted a big building with a huge parking lot. A neon sign out front read, "The Ragged Ass Saloon." They pulled in and sat in the car for a minute, looking the place over. It was a one story wooden structure with a tin roof and wide porch that wrapped around the front and sides. Three battered tables, some old chairs and a few rockers were on the porch. "Features outdoor dining," Mary Rose said.

"Hey," Robbie said. "I'm not going anywhere without saying I ate in Resolution. Maybe somebody can scare us up a burger."

Inside it took a few minutes for their eyes to adjust. There were about twenty five big round tables with mis-matched chairs, a bar that could have been on a movie set of a cheap western, swinging doors leading to the kitchen, an old jukebox and four new wide-screen televisions.

"Afternoon, Ladies," a voice said from somewhere near the kitchen.

A tall, thin young man with blond hair that fell over his forehead came toward them. He wore cowboy boots, a plaid flannel shirt and jeans with a big turquoise belt buckle.

"Are you open?" Robbie asked.

"Sure," he said. "Sit anywhere. What can I get you?"

They ordered drinks and when he brought them to the table Maggie asked a surprising question, "Can I bring my dog in here? She's small and I hate leaving her in the car."

The other three looked at each other, *my dog*?

"Sure," the young man said. "Lots of animals come in here. Dog will be better than most."

When Maggie returned with Edith Ann the young man took her from Maggie's arms. "By damn," he said. "She's a little skinny thing. You just find her?" They nodded.

"Never went much for small dogs," he said. "Figured anything under 10 pounds was a squirrel in drag." His smile lit up his entire face. His eyes twinkled.

"We found her almost dead at our last campground," Hadley said. "Someone had shot her."

"Happens," he said. He looked at each of the ladies.

"You hungry?" He asked. They nodded. "We don't usually open the kitchen this early, but our cook is trying out some new things to see if we want 'em on the menu. You can judge the first attempt." He turned and yelled toward the kitchen, "Hey! We got some victims to try that new dish." He pulled up a chair between Robbie and Hadley and sat down.

"I'm Jimmie Sheen from Abilene," he said and offered his hand to them, one at a time. They told him their first names. "You here for long?"

"Kind of on an extended vacation," Maggie said.

"Do you have family here, Jimmie?" Hadley asked.

"Nope – free as a bird. Married to the Ragged Ass here. Always thought if I had a son though, I'd call him Keane. Then he'd be Keane Sheen from Abilene. Be like a boy named Sue – have to be tough to survive," he laughed and the sound reminded Robbie of music.

"Oh my God!" Mary Rose said and she pointed toward the ceiling. Hung with wooden clothes pins on a clothesline that encircled the entire huge room were all shapes and sizes of underpants. There were men's boxers and briefs in all colors, long underwear bottoms, women's old fashioned cotton panties, thongs, see-through briefs and a few crotchless pairs. "Feel free to contribute if you want," Jimmie said, smiling.

As they were turning their heads to look at underwear all around the room, a huge man exited the kitchen with a tray of steaming food, plates and silverware. His sparse hair was a greasy gray, his face hung in immense folds and Maggie swore she could feel the floor move as he walked. His arms were bigger than a pro football player's thighs. He must weigh at least 400 pounds, she thought.

"Hope ya'll like a little Cajun," he said as he sat the tray down in the center of the table. "I lived a few years in New Orleans.

"Cajun," Robbie said, "I have died and gone to heaven."

"This here's our chief cook and bottle washer," Jimmie said. "His first name is Henry and his last name is Domino, so guess what we call him." Jimmie's grin was from ear to ear.

The big man was smiling, too.

"Fats," Robbie said, "Gotta be Fats Domino after the famous singer." Both men nodded. "And you ladies would be...?" Fats said. They introduced themselves. Jimmie lifted Edith Ann up with one hand and held her up so they could introduce her as well.

The lake campground was beautiful with almost no other campers except on weekends when it filled up with boaters and people fishing. The girls frequented the Ragged Ass every night, going in early, sitting with Jimmie, talking with Fats and now and then pushing buttons on the old jukebox. Most days there were only four or five other customers that early, always men, leaning against the bar drinking beer and eating what Jimmie billed as, "Fats Famous Fries."

"We are gaining weight here, girlfriends," Robbie said one day. Since they had to walk Edith Ann, who was gaining weight faster than any of them, they just increased their distance and tried to up their speed.

Edith Ann was becoming beautiful. Her coat was

getting glossy, her eyes were shining, her gums were pink and healthy and she was obviously falling in love with Jimmie Sheen from Abilene and Fats Domino, who always saved some steak for her.

One Saturday afternoon, all five females were at their usual table trying out Fat's new meatloaf recipe when they heard a roar outside. Maggie stood and went to the front windows. "Sweet Jesus!" she exclaimed. "Jimmie, you better come here."

Everyone, including Fats, hurried to look. Outside, filling up the parking lot and still coming down the road were more than a hundred bikers.

"Oh man," Jimmie said. "What are we gonna do? They'll all want eats and drinks."

"I've got enough frozen hamburger and buffalo meat if we just serve 'em burgers," Fats yelled as he grabbed Hadley's hand and pulled her toward the kitchen and through the swinging doors. As the first bikers began to line up at the bar, all four women were tying aprons around their waists, Hadley was headed toward the grill to help cook and Jimmie was digging out order pads and pencils from beneath the bar. "I'll only have time to pour beer, no hard liquor," he yelled.

Two husky bikers in black vests stepped behind the bar.

"Tend bar in Denver," the first one said.

"Cheyenne," the other drawled and they began putting whiskey bottles within easy reach.

The jukebox bellowed, every table was filled with men and a few women, others were standing around the pool table and leaning up against the walls. There was a lot of laughter, some cussing and the noise reverberated off the wooden floors and walls. "Why God invented microwaves," Fats told Hadley as he threw in another package of hamburger to thaw. They were keeping up, but just barely. Maggie, Robbie and Mary Rose were nearly running from table to table. Fat's Fries were going to run short, but he had just sliced enough onions for rings that would have lasted through the weekend. The first hour of hard work sped by and controlled chaos reigned. All at once they heard Mary Rose yell, "Six flat cows with yellow bricks. Long hots and big stinkys on the side."

"What the hell is that?" Fats asked.

"I think she wants six cheeseburgers with fries and rings," Hadley said.

Mary Rose appeared to pick up more burgers and beer. "I always wanted to say something like that," she grinned.

Things began to settle down about two hours into the evening. Voices were lower, more conversation was going on. The cash register was still cha-chinging and the credit card machine was still hot, but things were easier, smoother, more under control. Fats wiped the sweat off his forehead and Hadley splashed cold water on her face. They looked at each other and laughed.

Out in the saloon, Mary Rose was sitting at a table talking with three women in leather biking pants, Maggie was scurrying to another table with her burger order and Robbie was picking up a fresh pitcher of beer to take to a table where six men were laughing.

She sat the pitcher down and a big man in a blue-striped shirt and black vest grabbed her around the waist. "Hey Chocolate," he said. His grin showed two missing teeth and one ugly gold one. "Give me some sugar," and he pulled her down on his lap and began fondling and trying to kiss her. Robbie reached over, grabbed the pitcher of beer and emptied it over his head. He dropped her to the floor and yelled, "You don't do that to me, you black bitch!"

A younger man in a bright red t-shirt and Nebraska cornhuskers cap stood up and smashed his fist into blue shirt's nose. Blood spurted out and blue shirt turned from Robbie and returned the punch.

Robbie stood up and stepped back as a chair was overturned at the table behind her. Pool balls began flying, a pool cue broke over someone's head, glass broke and the whole room was on its feet yelling and swinging. As Robbie turned toward the kitchen, a big man in a black muscle shirt took a swing at an equally big man with a Denver Broncos cap. Broncos cap ducked and the punch hit Robbie square in the temple.

She spun around. Her ears began to ring, she saw Maggie break a beer bottle over the head of a fat man in a Harley-Davidson cap, saw Hadley grab Maggie's wrist and pull her away while pushing Mary Rose toward the ladies room. Edith Ann was scampering along behind them as fast as her little legs would carry her. Mary Rose was looking over her shoulder and Robbie could tell she was calling her name, but she couldn't hear anything. Even the yelling and smashing and hitting had no sound. The room was weaving, too, and getting dimmer, like Jimmie had turned the lights down.

She dropped to her knees and crawled under the table nearest her. As she put her head down on the floor, the strong

smell of beer, onions and ketchup filled her nostrils. The
floor was sticky and black with years of built-up dust, dirt
and smoke. "We really need to scrub this floor," was her last
thought before she passed out.

## *Parker Roberts*

The first thing Robbie heard from under the table was a
gunshot, then something heavy hit the table above her and
glass shattered on the floor next to her. Robbie opened her
eyes. Was somebody shooting at dogs again? The bastards!
She heard a deep voice say, "Put what you owe on the table
boys, then move ass outta here. Fun's over." She heard hurried
footsteps that made her head spin again, then there was
blessed quiet and Jimmie was pulling her out from under the
table and setting her on a chair.

"You all right, Robbie?" he asked. He looked so worried
it made her smile.

"Ummm hun," she said.

Hadley, Maggie, Mary Rose and Fats were standing in
front of her. Edith Ann was burrowed into Mary Rose's arms,
her eyes wide. Standing in the middle of them was a big man
in Lucasie boots with brown pants, a brown shirt with a white
undershirt showing at the neck and a beat-up Stetson hat. A
badge was on his left shirt pocket and he was holstering a gun.

She worked at focusing.

"Sorry about the light, Jimmie," he said.

Jimmie shrugged. "Got their attention, Parker."

"It was collaterative damage," Parker said.

"Collateral," Jimmie said. The big man in brown nodded.

If you had taken Tom Selleck, put a thousand-pound weight on his head and pushed him down three inches this would be your man. He was stocky with a thinning brown mustache, narrow eyes, and a face lined with grooves that showed years of tough wear and tougher weather. "This is our sheriff," Jimmie said, "Parker Roberts."

Robbie focused best she could and squeaked, "Parker Roberts?"

The sheriff touched the brim of his hat.

"From *Appaloosa*?" she asked.

"He's from here," Jimmie answered.

"Resolution?" Robbie asked.

"Resolution is here," the sheriff said.

She looked at Parker Roberts. "Did you ever read *Appaloosa*, the book?"

"Not much for readin.'"

"See the movie?"

"Not much for movies, either."

'You've never heard of Robert Parker, the famous writer?"

"I have not."

"This is weird," Robbie said.

"It is," the sheriff said.

Robbie thought she was doing a pretty good job of holding her own. She looked hard at the sheriff, who was looking around the saloon, seeing everything. He appeared to be slow in every move, but Robbie instinctively knew he was faster than anyone. No one was faster. She had read all of Robert Parker's westerns. She loved Virgil Cole, his strong, quiet hero and she knew who was standing in front of her. "You can't fool me!" she said, and threw up on the floor.

# Muddy Ink

Robbie woke up the next morning with only a few bruises and no noticeable damage. She felt good and she had a mission. By the time Jimmie showed up to unlock the Ragged Ass all four women were waiting in the rockers on the big wrap-around porch. Stacked near the door were mops and buckets and several bags from the local hardware.

"Jimmie," Robbie began. "I'm sorry about last night. If I hadn't dumped the beer on that weirdo's head this wouldn't have happened."

"No way, Robbie," Jimmie said. "Wasn't your fault. What's up, ladies?" He glanced at the bags, mops and buckets.

"We're cleaning this pig-sty up, son," Maggie said, and led the way inside as soon as he opened the door. When everyone was in, she reached up and changed the "Open" sign Jimmie had just turned around back to "Closed."

By four o'clock they were done. Jimmie and Fats stood by the bar and watched Maggie turn the closed sign around. Hadley and Robbie were putting cleaning supplies in the saloon storage closet and Mary Rose was sweeping the porch.

"We have been visited by the church ladies from hell," Fats said.

"We have indeed," Jimmie grinned.

"Should I pour some whiskey on the floor to make it smell like home?"

"It'll get there soon enough," Jimmie said.

Fats looked up at the clothesline strung around the wall just beneath the ceiling. "They washed our underwear didn't they?"

Jimmie grinned wider. "In your kitchen sink and then hung 'em up to dry."

"Christ on a crutch," Fats said. "This is awful. I hope they didn't starch and iron 'em!" And he stomped out through the swinging doors to the kitchen.

Jimmie grinned some more.

The floor was so clean it had turned a lighter brown. The bar glistened, the glass behind it and the shelves holding the bottles sparkled along with the big front windows looking out on the parking lot and road. The polished tables and chairs reflected light from the overhead lighting and on the center of each table was a round placemat holding a votive candle in a glass holder. Robbie began making the rounds, lighting each one.

The whole place smelled clean as well – a breath of bleach and scouring powder and window cleaner made worse yet by the apple cinnamon room spray Mary Rose was wielding like a deadly weapon.

"Okay, girls," Jimmie yelled. "Time to rest your rears and get some food. Dinner's on me. I thank you. Last time that floor was washed was when the road flooded about fifteen years ago. It does look different in here, smells different, too." He motioned them to a table and sat with them. They were sweaty and dusty, their clothes smudged and dirty. Mary Rose's hair had splotches of something indescribable and as soon as they sat down and looked at one another they got up in pairs and headed for the ladies room to wash up. By the time they finished, Fats had buffalo steaks and baked potatoes in front of them along with big, frosty glasses of ice water.

"You didn't need to do this," Jimmie said. "You really

didn't, but while you were working your asses off here at the Ragged Ass, I made a phone call. I have a little present for you – a kind of thank you and an apology for what happened last night," Edith Ann sat on his lap while he gave her tiny pieces of his steak.

Jimmie went on. He seemed unusually happy to Maggie. Like there was something funny about to happen, some joke she didn't know about yet.

As they were talking, a shadow fell across their table. Standing beside them was another very big man. This one had tattoos from his wrists to the top of his oversized muscle shirt. A dragon tattoo wrapped around his neck. Hadley looked at his legs and was relieved to see he was wearing long pants. It took a minute to get past the ink to his black beard, shaved head and long, angular face. She couldn't see his mouth. His beard was complimented by a long, handlebar mustache. He must have been six feet four or five inches, and weigh over three hundred pounds, all muscle.

"Ladies," Jimmie said. "Meet Muddy Ink, our local tat artist and piercer."

Muddy pulled up a chair and sat down. Fats brought him a beer and a burger.

"Here's the deal," Jimmie smiled. "You four are family now. You're locals here in Resolution and I want you to be a real part of the Ragged Ass family. I want you to have something to remember us by when you move on." His grin was one Maggie hadn't quite seen before and his eyes had a mischievous twinkle that made him look about eight years old.

"I've contracted with Muddy here to give each of you the tattoo of your choice," he said. "My gift." And he slapped his hand down on the table, grinned wider still and looked at them. Maggie saw him give a quick wink to the giant sitting next to her.

"Oh, no way!" Mary Rose said.

"Not for me," Robbie said.

"You're kidding," Hadley said.

Maggie looked at Jimmie. "We'll do it," she said. Then she looked at each one of the Boob girls intently, rolling her eyes toward Jimmie ever so slightly. His big grin diminished for just a second then came back.

"We'll do it," she said again and gave all three women another look.

Hadley Joy looked at Maggie, then Jimmie, then Muddy. She began to smile a sly smile. "I always kind of wanted a tattoo," she said.

Robbie caught on, "I have a friend who has a little heart on her left breast," she said. "I always admired that."

Mary Rose stared at them.

All at once Muddy broke into a big grin. He had nice teeth and a smile that was unusually attractive. His voice was surprisingly high and soft for such a big body. He looked at Jimmie. "Jimmie," he said. "that is one damn nice thing you're doin' for these classy ladies. Nobody with this much style has ever been in my tat parlor."

Jimmie wasn't grinning anymore. It was as if he was adding figures and costs in his head.

# A Little Something for the Girls

Hadley drove the Hummer into town the next morning for their appointment with Muddy Ink.

"Are we actually going to do this?" Robbie asked.

"Why not?" Hadley said.

"Nothing to lose, a tattoo to gain," Maggie said.

Mary Rose stared at them.

Muddy's directions took them to the beautiful big Queen Ann Victorian they had noticed their first day in town. "This doesn't look like a tattoo place," Mary Rose said. They got out of the Hummer and walked up the steps to the big porch, Edith Ann leading the way. There was a small, tasteful sign on the big, oval-glassed door. *Muddy Ink Inc. Tasteful Tattoos and Painless Piercings.*

"Very nice," Hadley said.

"Very tasteful," Mary Rose said.

"Very my gawd isn't this interesting," Robbie said

"Very open," Maggie said, and she opened the door and walked in.

The house was decorated in period antiques, spotless and had the look of a well-kept museum.

"When I from my bed did rise, behold – I found this day a new surprise, and when the shock I did dismiss, said with wonder, 'what is this?" Robbie quoted from a poem she had written years ago when her husband had placed a bouquet of daisies on their dining room table and fixed breakfast for the two of them.

"This, my dear ladies, is my home," Muddy said, walking in to the parlor with a silver tray and porcelain coffee cups. "My educated guess is three decafs and one regular, am I right?" He motioned them into the second front parlor which had a dining table with walnut chairs and antique furniture that Hadley estimated at somewhere north of priceless.

He sat the tray on the table, disappeared for less than a minute and returned with another tray, this one filled with pastries and napkins that matched the cups.

"Muddy, this is awesome," Hadley said. "How did you come by this house?"

"My great-grandmother built it," Muddy said. "She pretty much built the town, too. Around the year 1890 Resolution was on a cattle trail. Herds would water at the lake. My great-grandmother was married to a wife-beater and she resolved to get away – that's where the town got its name, Resolution, after her resolve." He poured coffee from silver pots. A matching sugar and creamer sat filled on the tray.

"She ran off with his horse and buggy, what money they had and headed east. She spotted this place, knew about the trail drives, and pitched a tent. Within a year she had built a saloon, which is the bank now, and this house. Now this house has 10 rooms upstairs. We have a cattle trail, a saloon and….." he paused and smiled.

"A house of ill repute," Robbie finished.

"You got it," Muddy said. "She, like you, was a classy lady, a caring Madam and a beauty. She lured one of the biggest, meanest cattle foremen away from the herds and made him sheriff. Lots of their family still around, all descended from a madam and a sheriff." He pulled four big books out of a chest nearby and laid them on the table. "You met my brother, Fats, at the Ragged Ass," he went on. "Different fathers."

The coffee was delicious, the pasties fine, and Muddy opened the books to show page after page of tattoos.

"You really going through with this?" Muddy asked. "You know Jimmie was foolin' with you don't you?" They nodded.

"But hey, why not? Hadley said.

"I'd do a rose on my breast," Robbie said, "but at the rate I'm sagging it would be a long-stem in a month or so."

Hadley had an idea. "Muddy," she said, "could you do something like a couple of daisies that would sort of take the shape of boobs? Something to symbolize us – we call ourselves The BOOB girls."

"BOOB girls?" Muddy said. His eyebrows went up to the middle of his forehead and without thinking, he glanced at their chests.

"Burned Out Old Broads," they said together.

Muddy reached into a drawer and pulled out a legal pad and pen. He began to draw. After a minute or two he turned the pad around for them to see.

Drawn in pink and yellow was what resembled two small bouquets of daisies that protruded just a bit, giving it a three dimensional affect of very small flower breasts.

"I like it," Hadley said.

"Cool," Robbie said.

"I like it, too," Mary Rose said.

"I'm first," Maggie said.

The actual tattoo studio was in the back of the house. It was clean and neat and comfortable. They all watched as Muddy went to work on Maggie's chest, just above her bra line. She asked him how much it would cost to wrap a bull snake around her navel and letter "Methuselah" in a circle around it. He told her and she made an appointment.

Hadley's tattoo went to the same spot above her bra, but Mary Rose and Robbie had their tattoos on their hips just above what would have been a bikini line.

They talked and laughed. Muddy told them more about Resolution and how it grew then became a town dependent on tourism to the lake when the cattle ran out. They took a lunch break and Muddy had sandwiches made and lemonade ready.

"Tell you what," Muddy said. "If you'll show 'em to Jimmie, I'll give you all navel rings for free." They laughed.

"Nothing to lose and a ring to gain," Maggie said.

By four o'clock they were ready to go to the Ragged Ass. Maggie and Muddy led the way on his Harley Fat Boy motorcycle. Robbie pointed through the windshield at Maggie. She was in the bitch seat behind Muddy, sitting with her arms high and straight in the air, head back, eyes closed, hair flying.

"Free at last, free at last," Robbie said. "Praise God almighty, I am free at last."

The usual regulars were gathered at the bar. Muddy led the way in. "Jimmie! Fats! Come here!" he yelled. Jimmie and Fats came out of the kitchen to where Muddy and the ladies were standing at the end of the bar.

"My best artwork yet," Muddy said, and he spread one arm toward the women. As practiced, Hadley and Maggie pulled their shirts open and their left bra down just enough to show their tattoos. At the same time, Robbie and Mary Rose bent over, pulled their jeans and panties down just enough to show their daisy bouquets.

"And the finishing touch," Muddy bellowed, and in

one move they opened their jeans and pulled up their shirts to show their navel rings.

There was total silence.

Jimmie stared with his mouth open. "Jeezus!" he whispered.

Fats began to smile. "Little brother, you have done fine, fine work here. Tonight drinks and dinner are on me," and he turned and went through the swinging doors to the kitchen. They could hear him laughing, then he stuck his head through the doors. "Remember, girls," he bellowed. "I lived in New Orleans and there we say, 'Show me your tits!'" The doors swung shut and they could hear him laughing for a long time.

## A Nice Walk Around the Lake

The Resolution Lake was massive. The paved paths along the shore stretched for more than six miles and provided a great walking and biking area. On a morning when the air was brisk and fresh, when the trees were filled with birds and fish were actually jumping in the lake, the BOOB girls put on their walking shoes and took off, Edith Ann running ahead of them, bounding into the woods and dashing to the lake to wade into the water and back out again.

They had talked now and then of moving on, but Resolution was beginning to feel like home. They liked the town, they liked the quiet of the campground and they loved Jimmie, Fats and Muddy. Hadley had bought a good-sized grill at the hardware store and every Sunday the three younger men came for brunch, with Fats taking over the grill like the pro he was.

They had a large movie collection, enjoyed sitting

outside reading, sang in horrendous harmony when they cleaned the trailer and found a welcome and surprising contentment in their lives. There was routine and permanence. Now the bunk beds belonged to Robbie and Maggie and ever since the first week on the road, Hadley and Mary Rose had taken over the queen-sized bed in the big bedroom.

Robbie thought on all these things as they walked beside the lake. She thought how we don't always find our families in the home where we are born. She thought about how home really was where the heart was and that could change as life changed. And as always, she thought about her husband and the love they had shared.

Mary Rose broke into those thoughts,.

"I have to go pee," she said. "I always hate it when I have to go outside, I always get my panties wet."

"Take 'em off," Maggie said.

Mary Rose shrugged. "I'm headed for the woods, girls. Walk slow."

"We should get one of those bird books and see what all these chirpers are about," Maggie said. They stopped to listen for a minute as a tree came alive with small, colorful birds who raised their voices to serenade the lake.

Suddenly Mary Rose burst out of the trees at a run. She was waving her arms and yelling. "I peed on a foot!" she yelled. "I peed on a foot!"

Hadley smiled at her. "It's okay, Mary Rose, just run on down to the lake and wash it off."

"No!" Mary Rose said loudly. "No!"

"Mary Rose, honey," Robbie said, "They're walking

shoes. We can throw them into the laundry when we get back."

Mary Rose grabbed Robbie by both arms and shook her a little. "No!" she said again. "It wasn't my foot! There's a dead body in the woods!"

The body wasn't even buried. It was carefully covered with piles of leaves and topped with branches that had been broken or cut from near-by trees. When Mary Rose had turned, squatted and urinated, she had washed some of the leaves away. Beneath them was a man's loafer, complete with foot inside.

"Oh my God," Hadley said,

"Sweet Jesus," Robbie said.

"Jesus, Mary and Joseph," Mary Rose said.

"This is not a prayer meeting, ladies. We need to get help." Maggie said.

Edith Ann had run along behind them and sniffed at the leaves. Hadley bent down to remove a branch when Edith Ann jumped over it, ran a few feet from the where the head would be, faced the woods and growled a deep, menacing snarl.

"Listen!" Maggie hissed. "Somebody's coming."

They were quiet. Edith Ann continued to growl and coming closer by the minute, they could hear footsteps crackling leaves and branches on the ground.

Edith Ann barked. The footsteps stopped.

They listened.

Silence.

Edith Ann growled and barked again.

Nothing.

"If it was just somebody walking along, they'd keep coming," Hadley whispered.

"The killer!" Robbie said.

Hadley grabbed Edith Ann, who looked behind them from Hadley's arms and barked again. She was still growling.

"Haul ass, girls!" Maggie said. They hauled ass.

They hit the path running as fast as they could and made it almost a quarter of a mile before they ran out of breath.

"Oh geez," Maggie said, puffing. "Who has the cell phone?"

"We never carry the cell phone," Hadley said. "We've never used it."

"There's a phone in the Hummer," Robbie remembered.

They walked as fast as they could. A curve in the path had taken them well out of view of the spot where Mary Rose had found the body. Maggie and Hadley broke into a fast trot. Robbie stopped and put her hand on her heart. "I have to slow down, girls." She said.

"I'll come with Robbie," Mary Rose said.

Hadley and Maggie climbed into the Hummer in the lake parking lot.

"How do you work the thing?" she asked.

"Damned if I know," Maggie said. She rummaged through the glove compartment, the console and the pocket in the door, finally coming up with a manual.

"RTFM" she said. "Read The Frigging Manual."

Hadley thumbed through the pages and after fumbling a few times, found instructions for the phone. She talked

Maggie through bringing the screen up and Maggie touched 9-1-1. As the phone was ringing in the sheriff's office, Robbie and Mary Rose piled in the back seat.

"Who did you call?" Robbie asked.

"The sheriff," Hadley said. "Parker Roberts."

"Parker Roberts?" Robbie said her eyes wide.

"You know," Mary Rose said. "You met him the night of the fight at the Ragged Ass."

"Oh," Robbie said. "Yeah, I know. But I thought he was a hallucination."

The sheriff's cruiser pulled in beside them in less than 5 minutes.

"Advantages of a small town," Hadley said.

Parker Roberts got out of his car and met them as they were climbing out of the Hummer. "Where is it?" he said. They pointed down the path.

"About a mile that way, in the woods," Maggie said.

"Get in," he said, and motioned to his cruiser.

Parker drove slowly down the path around the lake, two wheels on the pavement and two on the grass. After nearly a mile, he stopped and looked at the women, his eyebrows raised in a question.

"I think it's about here," Mary Rose said.

"Maybe a little farther up?" Hadley said.

"Not sure," Robbie said.

Maggie got out of the car and everyone followed her over the grass and into the trees.

"Not here," she said.

"You didn't check for a landmark, did you?" Parker sighed.

They went through the woods for a good fifteen

minutes, then walked out again to the path and looked both ways at the trees.

"It really was here!" Mary Rose said.

"Don't doubt it," the sheriff said.

Farther down the path they could see a young couple coming toward them, a German shepherd bouncing along by their side. As they watched, the big dog raised his head, sniffed the air and ran into the woods.

The sheriff looked at the girls then back toward the spot from where excited and enthusiastic barking was echoing through the woods. "Found it," Parker said.

When they got to the spot where Mary Rose had found the body, the dog was digging joyously. Leaves were flying and the young man was fumbling around the dog trying to get a leash hooked onto his collar.

They looked at the ground for a good minute in disbelief.

"It's gone!" Mary Rose said.

The body had disappeared.

Parker sent the young couple on their way and squatted beside the pile of leaves and brush, his big forearms resting on his knees, his hat tipped back. He looked for a long time. Robbie knew he was seeing everything.

"Been here," he said.

He scooped some of the leaves aside where the chest would have been.

"Blood," he said.

"Do you think he was shot?" Hadley asked.

"I do."

He walked around to the other side of the make-shift

grave, and squatted again, his arms in the same positions. "Not very tall," he said.

Maggie had a firm grip on Edith Ann, who was wiggling to get down and do her own digging.

They told Parker how Mary Rose had found it, including why she went into the woods in the first place. They told him about hearing someone coming and the sheriff walked through the trees in that direction for several minutes. When he came back, he circled the pile of leaves one more time. Near where the foot had been uncovered he knelt down and picked something up from under the leaves that had flown around when the shepherd was digging.

"Don't really need these for evidence," he said, and handed Mary Rose her panties. Then he looked at Hadley, smiled and winked. She smiled back.

## J. Frederick Sapp

There was no word about the body, no gossip they could uncover at the Ragged Ass, no contact with the sheriff. Life went on as usual.

One day Maggie dropped the other three off at the Ragged Ass and drove into town to have the oil changed and the Hummer checked out. The garage was known as Big Hal's and they had all liked him when they went in the day before to make an appointment.

Hal liked them too, and he loved the Hummer. He looked like he owned a garage. He was big, probably six four with a brown pony tail, a deep tan, triple pierces in his ears and tattoo chains around his big biceps. He wore a baseball hat backward on his head and was dressed in brown work pants, a muscle shirt and heavy duty boots. His hands were dirty, his clothes were dirty and he looked like he worked hard and loved it. He would treat the Hummer like his own baby. Hadley, Robbie and Mary Rose helped Fats in the kitchen then sat in the big rockers on the porch and drank coffee while they waited for Maggie. Just before the four o'clock regulars started arriving, the Hummer drove into the parking lot followed by a Lincoln town car. Maggie jumped out of the Hummer and hurried to the town car. A small man, just taller than Maggie, stepped out and offered her his arm. They walked to the porch together. He looked to be in his late sixties.

Edith Ann jumped down from her curled-up comfort in Mary Rose's lap, ran behind the rocker and growled. Maggie was beaming. "Girls," she cooed, "this is J. Frederick Sapp. He's renting one of the lake cottages and we met at Hal's." She looked up at J. Frederick with sickening doe eyes. J. Frederick Sapp had a mass of thick, wavy white hair that should have been attractive but somehow wasn't. He wore a seersucker suit with a white shirt and string tie with a turquoise clip. His boots looked like real snake skin and Hadley did a quick glance from the boots to Maggie. She hadn't seemed to notice they held a close likeness to Methuselah. There were three big rings on his hands. Hadley's husband had one and he called it his 'pimp' ring.

J. Frederick took each woman's hand and touched it to his lips. He was here for a month, looking at properties. Retired. Bored. Came from Denver. Needed a change. Mary Rose brought him a cup of coffee and they made more small talk.

*Shoes and ships and sealing wax talk,* Robbie thought.

Maggie was looking at the man goo-goo eyed and almost bouncing up and down as he leaned against the porch rail, coffee cup in hand. She looked like an eight-year-old who had stolen another girl's Barbie doll. At any minute Robbie expected her to break into, "Finders keepers – losers weepers," and wave J. Frederick around in the air.

Hadley thought there was grayness about him, a hardness.

Mary Rose rocked in her rocker and stared. Edith Ann stared with her from behind the rocker.

Finally Maggie announced that Fred was going to show her his cabin. She grabbed his hand and led him off the porch. The other three watched them go. They walked slowly, their heads together in secret conversation.

"There was a big black NFL player named Sapp," Robbie said.

"Doubt they're related," Hadley said.

Mary Rose continued to stare.

J. Frederick Sapp walked with his head lurched forward and his shoulders slumped. His small pot belly hung out over his belt.

Robbie leaned over the arm of her rocker toward Hadley. "He don't know SHIT," she said. J. Frederick didn't straighten up his shoulders, lift his head or tuck in his tummy. He opened the passenger door of his car for Maggie and she crawled in.

"I just don't like him," Mary Rose said. Edith Ann came out from behind the rocker, jumped into Mary Rose's lap and watched the big car move out of the parking lot. She was trembling just a little.

Maggie had virtually disappeared. Some nights she didn't come home at all. When she was at the Ragged Ass, J. Frederick Sapp sat with them for a few minutes, never had a soft drink or a beer, then left. After two weeks, Fats and Jimmie and Muddy joined them at their table in the tavern.

"There's something funny about that dude," Muddy said.

"There is," Fats said.

"I don't like him," Mary Rose and Jimmie said together.

"We need to check him out," Fats said.

"Big Hal," Muddy said. Fats nodded.

"Hal? At the garage?" Robbie asked.

Fats and Muddy nodded again.

"He's a computer geek," Muddy said. "He may have grease under his fingernails, but those fingers can find out anything about anybody. Just give him a keyboard."

The three girls looked at each other. Anybody?

"Anybody?" Hadley asked.

"Sure," Fats said. "He's our brother."

"Different fathers," Muddy said.

The next time Maggie showed up for Sunday brunch at the trailer, everybody was there and the boys were ready and waiting. J. Frederick Sapp always had an excuse to avoid them. Maggie was alone and at their mercy.

As soon as she sat down, Edith Ann jumped onto her lap and licked her hands and face. Everyone else grabbed their lawn chairs and moved close in around Maggie.

"Maggie," Hadley said. "We have something you need to know." Fats began.

"Maggie," he said, "this dude, J. Frederick Sapp is no good. He's a gambler big time, been with a Chicago mob. He's a con man and has a sheet a mile long."

"A sheet means he's been arrested," Mary Rose said.

Maggie looked at her with narrowed, angry eyes. "I know what a sheet is," she said.

"Well, I didn't," Mary Rose said in her own defense.

"Hal researched him," Muddy said, "he's got a warrant out for assault in Illinois, he's been arrested for grand theft. He's a damn crook, Maggie, and get this, he's called Fast Buck Freddie in Chicago."

"We love you, Maggie," Robbie said. "All of us do and we' don't want you get hurt. This guy can hurt you big time. He's nothing but bad news."

"You aren't in love, Maggie," Hadley said. "You're besotted."

Maggie looked at each one of them. They had attacked her before Fats even started grilling the breakfast meat. She was surprised and hurt and confused. She opened her mouth to say something, closed it then stood up, dumping Edith Ann off her lap.

"You can all go to hell," she whispered. And she walked to J. Frederick Sapp's big town car and drove away.

There was an awkward silence.

"That went well," Jimmie said.

# Breakin' up is Hard to Do

Later that afternoon Maggie came slowly through the door of the Ragged Ass and walked to the table where the other three were drinking ice tea and lemonade.

"Fred and I broke up," she said. She buried her face in her hands and sobbed. "I really loved him," she squeaked. Hadley handed her a napkin. Mary Rose handed her a second one. Robbie slid a third across the table. Edith Ann stood up on Mary Rose's lap, put her front paws on the table, looked lovingly at Maggie and wiggled all over.

"He wasn't at the cabin when I got there," Maggie choked out the words, then she was quiet for a minute and an angry look crept across her face. "I logged on to his computer and checked where he'd been on the Internet. There were all kinds of porn sites and chat rooms with young girls and some crazy emails to Chicago and..." she was interrupted by gasps and sobs that came from deep in her chest. Maggie raised her index finger to signal for a minute's time to collect herself. She took a deep breath and went on. "It was terrible, sleazy, dirty stuff." She sighed and looked at them.

"I thought about all I'd lose if I left you three for him. You're family. You're my safety net. You're sure and solid and I don't want to ever lose you."

Fats brought her a frosty glass of tea. He stood beside her for a few seconds, then pulled her out of her chair, lifted her up and gave a gigantic hug, holding her close to his chest, her feet off the floor while she cried into his white cook's coat.

They went back to the trailer early, talking about a comedy movie to cheer them all up. When they stepped inside the trailer, Hadley stopped. "Something's wrong," she said. "Something's different." Edith Ann stopped beside her and growled a low growl.

A drawer was not quite shut. The couch, which made into a bed, had been pulled out and put back with a corner of a light afghan caught in it. "What's that smell?" Mary Rose asked.

Maggie snorted. "J. Frederick Sapp's New York City cologne."

Hadley hurried into the big bedroom and pulled up the bed. The trailer had a large, convenient storage area beneath the bed. Attached to a spring hinge, it was easily raised and lowered.

Inside were the four small suitcases they had brought with them. A clear space showed where a fifth had been.

"He took our money," Hadley said. "The bastard robbed us."

They stood and looked into the storage area as if they could make it reappear.

"What do we do?" Mary Rose said.

"Go get him and kill the sonovabitch," Maggie said.

"Do we need a plan?" Robbie asked.

"Do we need to call Parker?" Hadley asked.

"By the time Parker gets here Fred could be gone," Maggie said. "C'mon," and she went back out the door. The others followed her to the Hummer.

Maggie drove off the road to a woody area close to a small lake cottage and parked in the shadows of the trees. "That's his place," she said.

The cottage looked out on the lake and had a good-sized shed behind it. The town car was parked beside the shed. Just as Maggie turned the motor off, J. Frederick hurried out of the cottage, got into the town car and peeled out of the drive onto the road into town.

"Very convenient," Hadley said.

"Good timing," Robbie said.

"Good luck," Mary Rose said, and they piled out of the Hummer and hurried to the cottage, Edith Ann trotting along behind. Maggie produced a key and they were inside.

The cottage was dim and shadowy. Hadley turned on the lights and started looking in closets. Mary Rose looked in drawers and smaller places in case Fred had taken the money out of the suitcase and hidden it. Robbie walked around the cottage looking for outside hiding places. Maggie scoured the screened -in porch which was filled with furniture and junk. After several minutes they met inside. "Not here," Hadley said.

"The shed," Maggie said.

The shed had been used as a workplace and storage. There was a high work bench covered with tools and a collection of kerosene lamps with glass chimneys. Along one wall hung a large collection of cast iron cooking utensils. Shovels and rakes lined another wall. A lawnmower was in one corner and an eight-foot freezer was hooked up and purring against the far end of the shed. A single light bulb hung near the door. Robbie pulled on the chain and the light flickered on, casting shadows into the corners.

Edith Ann ran over and put her front paws up on the freezer.

"Freezer," Robbie said.

"Padlocked," Mary Rose noticed.

"Suspicious," Hadley said.

Maggie said nothing. She walked over and began playing with the combination on the padlock. In less than ten minutes it pulled open.

"For a Chicago crook he's not very smart. Used his birthday."

She opened the lid and they gathered around. The freezer was filled with packages wrapped in white freezer paper and taped shut with masking tape. Lying on top toward one end, as if it had been casually tossed in, was their suitcase.

Hadley leaned over the freezer, unzipped the suitcase and looked inside. "It's all there," she said and she lifted it out, gasped and jumped back, dropping the suitcase on the floor. The case had shifted some of the wrapped packages. Sticking out between some of them was a man's foot, wearing a loafer.

"It's the foot!" Mary Rose said.

"It's the body!" Robbie said.

"Fred's the killer." Maggie said.

"It's too late," Hadley said.

The town car had just pulled up beside the shed. Edith Ann began to bark.

"Shhhhh!" they all said together.

Fred got out of the car, saw the light on in the shed, heard Edith Ann's bark and drew a gun.

"Oh crap!" Maggie whispered. "I left my gun in Omaha."

"You have a gun?" Mary Rose said.

Hadley grabbed the biggest cast iron skillet from the rack on the wall and slipped behind the door. The other three pressed themselves against the freezer which still stood open.

Fred stepped inside the door.

"Ladies," Fred said, aiming the gun at Maggie. "You should have called first." He squinted against the dim light. Hadley took one step forward and smashed the cast iron skillet into his skull.

"Hey!" he yelled.

Edith Ann jumped up and sank her teeth into his arm just above the gun, letting out a growl that would do a Great Dane proud.

"Hey!" he yelled again, tried to shake her off and dropped the gun.

Robbie grabbed one of the kerosene lamps and hit Fred as hard as she could in the face, breaking the glass chimney. His nose began to bleed and glass shards embedded themselves in his cheeks and rained down on the floor. Maggie grabbed the gun.

Fred finally shook Edith Ann off his arm. She landed with a yelp and grabbed hold of his pant leg. Fred shook his leg and took a swing at Robbie. She ducked. Mary Rose took careful aim and kicked as hard as she could at his groin. The kick went wide and dislocated his knee cap.

"Hey!" he yelled again.

"Never did have much of a vocabulary," Maggie said, and she took hold of the gun barrel and hit him as hard as she could in the temple. There was a resounding crack.

This time Mary Rose was on target. Fred let out a

scream and bent over, his hands on his groin. "I always wanted to do that," Mary Rose gasped.

Hadley finished the job with three more head smashes with the skillet.

Robbie found a wooden rolling pin on the workbench and said, "One more time," and broke the thick part of the pin over his head.

J. Frederick Sapp was out cold at the feet of four panting women and a small growling dog.

They stood back and breathed hard.

"Is he dead?" Mary Rose asked.

Hadley reached down and felt a pulse in the big vein in his neck. "Just unconscious, may have a bit of a concussion though."

Maggie looked at them with a serious, worried look.

"Girls – I need to get out of here," she said. "I need to move on from Resolution."

They looked at her for a few seconds. None of them questioned her.

"First let's take care of J. Frederick," Hadley said. "Do we call Parker?"

"I don't think so," Robbie said and she looked at Maggie with great tenderness.

"We can't just leave him here. He might come after us," Mary Rose said.

"Jimmie?" Robbie said.

"Too innocent, too honest," Hadley said.

"Muddy," Maggie and Mary Rose said together.

Maggie went to the Hummer to call Muddy. The other three talked together, leaning over Fred's limp body. Hadley grabbed Fred under his shoulders. Robbie and Mary Rose each took a leg and they pulled, lifted and drug him out of the shed, over the grass and into the cottage bedroom.

Maggie came hurrying through the door. "Muddy's on his way."

Maggie grabbed one arm, Hadley the other and with Robbie and Mary Rose doing the leg work, the four BOOB girls tried to lift Fred onto the bed. He didn't budge. They tried a second time. His worthless skinny ass seemed to be glued to the floor.

"Should we try lifting him from under his butt and shoulders?" Mary Rose asked.

"Maybe if we swung him," Robbie said.

"He's not that big," Maggie added. "We should be able to swing him up there."

They grabbed hold of both arms and both legs and started swinging Fred back and forth, "On three," Maggie gasped. "One – Two – THREE!"

J. Frederick Sapp flew up onto the bed, rolled over it and landed on the floor on the other side.

"Shit! Shit! Shit!" Maggie said.

"Let's take a break," Robbie said. "You think he has any pop in the refrigerator?"

They looked at her.

"Okay," she said, and moved around to the other side, grabbing a leg as soon as she got there.

"One – Two – THREE!" Maggie said again.

This time Fred cooperated and landed neatly on his back in the middle of the bed.

"In mysteries, this is where we secure the victim so we can escape." Hadley said.

"This is like a bad episode of 'Murder, She Wrote'," Robbie said.

"There were no bad episodes of 'Murder, She Wrote'," Mary Rose said.

Maggie went to the closet and dug around in a corner. She came out carrying two pairs of handcuffs. "Don't ask," she said.

They handcuffed Fred to the head of the bed. Mary Rose went to the kitchen and dug around until she found a full roll of masking tape like the kind binding the packages in the freezer and a pair of scissors.

They wrapped masking tape a dozen times around each ankle and the posts on each end of the foot of the bed. "Not as good as duck tape, but a girl's gotta do what a girl's gotta do," Mary Rose said as she made a large X over his mouth, repeated it six or seven more times then wrapped the tape around the back of his head and over his mouth again.

Maggie opened a drawer and drew out a pair of Fred's black bikini briefs. She walked to the head of the bed, lifted his head and slipped them down over his eyes with the leg holes on top. Some of his wavy white hair sprung out through the holes. "Makes it more romantic if he can't see."

Robbie checked his pulse again, looked up, raised her eyebrows, nodded and shrugged.

Muddy's truck rumbled into the drive. They heard his door slam and listened for his heavy footsteps to come through the cottage.

"Wow, isn't that interesting," he said as he reached the bedroom door. "Nice work." Edith Ann ran over to him and he picked her up.

"He took our money," Hadley said.

"He has a dead body in the freezer in the shed," Mary Rose said.

"He aimed a gun at Maggie," Robbie said.

"So for all of the above we beat the holy crap out of him," Maggie said.

"Nice work," Muddy said again. "Interesting."

"Mary Rose introduced his balls to his upper intestine," Maggie announced.

"Served him creamed nuts," Robbie added.

"Gonad goulash," Hadley said.

Muddy grimaced. "Ouch."

Maggie walked across the room and took Muddy's hand. "Muddy, we gotta leave here. We have to move on. I can't tell you all the reasons why, but it's best if we do. You've been family and we love you and we're just gonna let you take it from here. But we don't want you in any trouble over this. You got any ideas?"

Muddy thought for a few minutes.

"I do. Let's see if he has any pop in the refrigerator."


They found sodas and leaned against the kitchen cupboards. No one seemed to want to sit at Fred's table or in any of the chairs. There was a kind of quiet urgency about what they were doing.

"Parker's gotta know because of the body and because of the warrant out for him in Chicago," Muddy began. "I figure what happened here was some kind of a deal gone bad and it probably involved a prostitute…there are a few around here at the truck stop down the road. I'll stay with him until you get on your way, then I'll call Parker."

"He'll wonder why you're here," Hadley said.

"No prob," Muddy smiled. "I make house calls. He wanted two tattoos – one for himself and one for a lady."

"We'd better show you what's in the shed," Maggie said.

Muddy followed them out and surveyed the damage left over from the beating they had inflicted on J. Frederick. He looked at the foot in the freezer then at the glass on the floor, a quiet smile growing on his face. "Yep. Definitely kinky shed sex gone bad."

"Parker's going to believe that?" Hadley asked.

"I can take care of Parker," Muddy replied. "He's my brother. Different fathers."

They hugged Muddy goodbye. They kissed him and held his hands. He was actually getting teary as Robbie picked up Edith Ann and they walked out the door and through the trees to where the Hummer was parked. They climbed in and Maggie began to drive toward the road.

"Stop!" Hadley yelled. "My God, stop!"

Maggie slammed on the breaks. Mary Rose and Robbie both jumped in their seats. Hadley began to scramble out of the car, acting awkward and frightened.

"We forgot the money," she said, and she ran back toward the shed.

It didn't take long to hook up the trailer. The slide outs were in, the hoses disconnected and drained, the electric cord wound into its holder. Dishes and all loose things were secure and ready for travel. As they did a last walk through and double check, Hadley spoke. "There's one last thing we need to do, girls," she said. She went into the bedroom, pulled out a drawer and brought out a flowered gift bag filled with pink tissue paper. They all smiled.

Their one stop on the way out of town was at the Ragged Ass. The early dinner crowd was beginning to fill the parking lot as Robbie drove the Hummer and trailer around to the back door. They got out and went into the familiar-smelling kitchen. There would be buffalo steak and buffalo burgers tonight.

"Hey girls," Fats said.

Maggie went to the swinging doors and motioned for Jimmie to come into the kitchen from behind the bar.

"What's up, ladies?" Jimmie said. He was drying his hands on a bar towel.

They took turns telling them they had to leave and what each had meant to them. Like Muddy, Fats got teary and sniffled once or twice. It had been a grand friendship and neither man pressed them for reasons for their leaving. They had been older sisters to Fats and Muddy and surrogate mothers to Jimmie. It was simple and direct and real. They all loved each other.

They promised to keep in touch and knew they probably wouldn't. They would keep memories and good times and know they were better people for having cared deeply.

Hadley handed Jimmie the flowered bag. The pink tissue paper stuck out of the top. "We didn't have a card to go with it," she said. "If we had, it would just say, 'thank you'." She turned, gave a little finger wave and walked out the door. The other three did the same, and in less than a minute Jimmie and Fats heard the big Hummer move out of its spot behind the kitchen.

Jimmie turned to the pink bag sitting on the counter. Fats moved over to look. Jimmie pulled out the contents and both began to grin. Inside were three pair of spandex tummy-control panties, one pair black, one white, one brown along with one pair of plain white cottons, size small and at the very bottom of the bag was a red thong with the Target store price tag still attached.

# PART 3:

# *Polly, Pornography and One Big Indian*

*If dreams exceed expectations,
how can we overly grieve them when they end?*

Dean Koontz

They drove for about two hours, found a campground and stopped, leaving the trailer hooked up to the Hummer so they could move on as soon as they got around in the morning. They were bone tired.

As soon as the slides were out and the trailer set up, Mary Rose poured four sodas and they sat around the table.

"We need to talk about it," Robbie said. "We gave Freddie one hell of a beating."

"We did good," Maggie said.

"I've never done anything even close to that in my entire life," Hadley said.

"Made me feel like Wonder Woman, without the costume," Mary Rose said.

"We are so good, we can leave the costume at home," Maggie said.

"Think we should be traumatized by it?" Robbie said, "We almost killed him – might have actually."

"You feel traumatized?" Maggie asked, looking around at the other three.

"Nope."

"Not me."

"No."

"I feel like popcorn and a movie," Mary Rose said, and she started throwing bags of popcorn into the microwave. Hadley started going through the CD album where they kept their movies. "How does *Thelma and Louise* sound?"

They slept late the next day then headed the Hummer south and west toward the Pacific Ocean. At a super-sized truck stop they talked over omelets and pancakes.

"I can't do a lot of mountain stuff," Robbie said, "my heart acts up."

"I always wanted to take a cruise," Mary Rose said.

"Lots of cruises from about anywhere on the coast," Hadley said.

"Suits me if we've got money for it," Maggie said.

"We have a lot," Hadley said, "I counted it this morning to see if Fast Buck Freddie had kept any, and we really haven't spent much. Jimmie fed us most of the time and campgrounds have been cheap."

"Go West young women, go West," Maggie said. They got a box for what was left of their omelets. Edith Ann would have a good supper.

The weather was perfect. They listened to Wolff Blitzer and music from the 50's and 60's on the Hummer radio. Robbie read aloud now and then from a book of poetry.

"What would have happened if Frost had taken the road most traveled?" Hadley wondered out loud.

"Would have ended up at a country club in Phoenix instead of the Ragged Ass," Robbie said, "we're the ones who have promises to keep and miles to go before we sleep."

"What promises will you keep, Robbie?" Mary Rose asked.

"I promise to live with a sense of humor," Robbie replied.

"I promise to enjoy how I look as I get older," Mary Rose said.

"I promise to live with grace, humor, courage and confidence," Hadley said.

"I promise to get into as much damn trouble as I can," Maggie said.

Every one of those promises would be kept.

# Polly Panchero

It was well outside a city on the coast when they found the campground they wanted. It had a mountain view, a lot of trees, a small lake and spacious campsites. The campground was larger than the one in Resolution. It also had a small restaurant and grocery store.

Just minutes away was another huge truck stop, and they could hear trucks humming along the highway all night. The sound was comforting to Maggie and Hadley. Mary Rose and Robbie had trouble sleeping through the night because of it.

The second day, while Robbie was researching cruises from the city near them on the Internet and not finding any leaving port soon, Hadley looked around the trailer. Maggie was curled up on the couch with a book and Mary Rose was in the campground laundry room. "Did Mary Rose take Edith Ann with her?"

They looked at each other, then looked around the trailer as if the little dog would suddenly appear.

"I'll go check," Maggie said, and she stepped out of the trailer and hurried to the laundry room. In just minutes she was back. "She doesn't have her and I didn't see her outside." They all hurried from the trailer. Mary Rose was hurrying toward them from the laundry room. They spread out and started calling for Edith Ann.

A young woman stuck her head out of the trailer next door. It was an old 19-foot Airstream, with no slideouts and simple hookups. She was wearing jeans and a flannel shirt and dirty white sneakers. Her face showed marks of past teenage acne and her blonde hair was pulled up into a ponytail.

"I think I have her," she said. Nestled in the crook of one arm, looking happy as a clam, was Edith Ann. "She came to my door, and when I opened it, she jumped right in. This is the most loving little dog I've ever seen." She had a soft, easy southern accent.

Her smile was beautiful. "A smile to make the sun stand still," Robbie quoted to herself. Edith Ann was not anxious to get out of her arms.

"I'm Polly," the young woman said, "how ya'll doin'?"

Mary Rose headed back to the laundry room and Polly invited the others to join her at her picnic table for a glass of lemonade, fresh out of the can. The table was covered with a red and white checkered plastic tablecloth. A potted red geranium sat in the center in full bloom. Hadley noticed the curtains in the trailer's kitchen windows matched the checkered cloth.

Polly Panchero was a waitress at the truck stop down the road. She was sweet and funny and had a great laugh. Edith Ann never left her side and Polly kept up a continuous rubbing, patting and loving the dog.

"My big deal right now is school," she said. "I'm at the university with two classes this semester. That makes me a genuine sophomore."

"Where are you from, Polly?" Robbie asked.

"Georgia. I ran away from home when I was sixteen. My momma was a druggy, my old man was mean as dirt. I stole enough money from Momma's drug money and Daddy's wallet to buy a bus ticket to Colorado and walked in on my granny. She took me in, chased my daddy off when he came lookin' for me, and gave me enough money for my truck and trailer." She pointed to a faded red 1990 Ford 150 pickup parked in front of the trailer. One door had been replaced and never re-painted. "Growls like a mountain lion and I have to get in through the back door then climb over the front seat, but she runs like a wildcat and I'm attached to her. One of the truckers at the truck stop's gonna paint the door but I have to pay him first." For just a second her eyes looked sad and she turned them toward Edith Ann.

The next morning Polly showed up at the door just before her noon shift. Edith Ann was in her arms again. "I don't for the life of me know how she escapes."

Robbie opened the door and took Edith Ann. Polly was in her truck stop uniform, dressed like a country girl with a white peasant blouse, brown and white checked pinafore and white apron. Her name tag read, 'Hey Miss.' Robbie saw it, smiled and pointed at it.

"It's what everybody I'm serving yells when they want me, HEY MISS! So I made it my name."

They heard Polly's old truck come rumbling down the campground road and sputter to a stop next door every night about ten o'clock. They had lemonade with Polly almost every afternoon when they were home and she came over for breakfast or coffee twice a week when she didn't have classes. "If you put her in a blue and white pinafore, gave her pigtails and red slippers she could go down the road with the Tin Man, Scarecrow and Cowardly Lion," Hadley said one day.

It was past midnight one weekend night when Edith Ann jumped up on the bed between Mary Rose and Hadley and barked. Mary Rose put the pillow over her head. Hadley turned over and pulled the sheet up past her ear. Edith Ann barked again, louder.

"Okay. So you have to go out," Mary Rose said. She slid out of bed and slipped into her bathrobe and slippers. That's when she heard loud voices outside by Polly's trailer. She went to the window over the sink and peered out.

Standing in front of Polly's trailer was a homely, round man wearing a long-sleeve Pittsburgh Steelers shirt, black pants and boots. He reminded Mary Rose of a bloodhound. She could see a bald spot on the top of his head reflecting the light from Polly's kitchen. She couldn't make out what they were saying, but he was obviously angry and Polly was obviously scared. Mary Rose took three steps to the door and turned on their outside lights. The voices stopped. She put Edith Ann's leash on, clutched her bathrobe closed over her chest and opened the door.

The man turned, saw her and started toward a dirty red pickup parked on the grass in front of Polly's, but not before he turned and slapped her hard.

Maggie heard Mary Rose and Edith Ann go outside and followed them, wearing just the long red underwear she used as pajamas. Polly was facing her trailer, crying softly, still in her waitress uniform. Mary Rose turned her around into a hug.

"Who was he?" she asked.

"Lionel Starkbetter. He's been after me ever since I moved here." She opened her door and Mary Rose and Maggie followed her inside.

Polly's trailer was tiny and spotless. The Airstream's roof was rounded, making it seem ever smaller. Mary Rose and Maggie sat down at the little table, letting Polly know they weren't leaving her alone. She stood for a minute then sat down beside Maggie. She sighed.

"I invite some of the truckers home sometimes. They're all nice men and I only do it when my tuition is due. I'm paying cash for my school, that's why I can only take two classes at a time." She looked defiant and proud at the same time. "They know what the money's for and they know I won't do anything weird or dirty. Mostly, they want a little sex and a lot of talk." She gave a weak laugh and wiped a tear away. "I'm not really ashamed of it," she whispered.

Mary Rose spoke up, "I have said it before and I'll say it again. A girl's gotta do what a girl's gotta do!"

Maggie looked at her in surprise. Polly turned and looked at Maggie.

"I have led a completely pure life and am shocked and shook."

Polly looked at her harder and then began to laugh. The other two joined in.

"So who is this jerk Starkbetter?" Maggie asked.

"He has the local porno shop in the strip mall next to the truck stop. Sometimes when a trucker is visiting he sneaks up and tries to look in the bedroom window. If he can catch me coming in late, like tonight, he wants me to have sex with him and he threatens me and calls me names." She gave a little shiver. "He says he'll catch me at the right time and rape me, except he doesn't say it as polite as that."

Mary Rose thought Polly looked about forty years old right then. "How old are you Polly?"

"I'm twenty. I'm a sophomore."

# Lionel Starkbetter

"So Polly turns a trick or two for truckers," Hadley said.

"You could call 'em, Trucker Tricks,'" Maggie said.

They were sitting around their table telling Hadley and Robbie what had happened the night before. They were in their bathrobes with mugs of hot tea labeled Total Comfort. A soft, gentle rain was pattering on the rubberized roof of the trailer, giving an easy relaxation to the morning. Maggie thought how if you ever wanted contentment in life it was sitting with your soul sisters, your hands around a hot mug of tea and hearing rain on the roof.

"I've read about girls prostituting for tuition," Robbie said, "She could be Polly the Prostitute."

Mary Rose looked at Hadley, "You could be Hadley the Hooker."

Hadley smiled back, "We could have Sarah the Slut."

"Tillie the Tart," Maggie said. She shook her head, "nobody's named Tillie anymore. So what are we going to do about this Lionel Starkbetter?"

"We could beat him to a bloody pulp like we did J. Frederick Sapp," Mary Rose suggested.

"Our kitchen utensils aren't strong enough," Hadley said.

"We have four Dunkin' Donuts plastic mugs and my groin kick is deadly."

"That would make us kicking muggers," Robbie said. There was silence.

"We could put him out of business," Mary Rose said. They looked at her. "I heard about what some church women did to a porno shop in Iowa."

They bent closer.

Lionel Starkbetter's shop opened at noon. The next morning at 11:45 the four women were standing outside looking at it. The wind blew papers of all sizes around the dirty parking lot, giving the whole place a dismal, unkept look.

They had eaten breakfast at the truck stop then driven across the truck entrance to the row of shops toward the back. It couldn't be called a strip mall, it was really just one long building divided into different stores or bays. There was a liquor store, a dollar store, a video rental place, an empty space with an old For Lease sign taped inside the window and then XXX-GIRLS Adult Emporium.

"Adult Emporium?" Robbie said.

"Upscale," Hadley said.

"Exclusive," Mary Rose said.

"Smelly," Maggie said.

There was the smell of diesel from the truck stop drifting over on the breeze, but the real odor came from an overflowing dumpster next to the liquor store. As they watched, a young man drove up in a mini-van and dumped a loaded black garbage bag on the pile that had already spilled out of the huge dumpster. "Your friendly neighborhood garbage dump," Maggie said.

They were all, including Maggie, wearing skirts and blouses, and comfortable but stylish shoes. Maggie had even applied a layer of lipstick and let Mary Rose use eyebrow pencil on her brows. As they waited, Lionel's red pickup rolled up to the shop and he got out.

The pickup had a detailed flame painted in yellow and orange from the front tires through the front doors in an attempt to give a picture of the wheels on fire. The windows were tinted and someone had written, "Wash me" in the dirt on the back of the truck bed. The girls walked across the parking lot and followed Lionel inside.

The porno shop was dim with poor lighting. It smelled of smoke and damp. An unidentified acidic smell hung in the air. Books were on shelves and in bins everywhere. There was a separate section for videos, booths for viewing them and a rack of magazines. The covers of some magazines were turned up from the dampness. Lionel held court behind an old cash register that stood on a counter in front of a black curtain that might have led to an office.

He looked surprised when he saw them. "What can I do for you ladies?"

"We're just browsing," Mary Rose said with a smile. Lionel looked doubtful.

"And shopping," Robbie said. "I love books."
Lionel Starkbetter was short, flabby and ugly. Mary Rose recognized the small bald spot on the top of his head when he turned away from them. He wore a black shirt with a pocket for cigarettes, black pants and black walking shoes. His eyes were dark and he once again made Mary Rose think of a bloodhound.

They wandered around the shop, picking up books, lifting up videos….browsing. Lionel watched them from a stool behind his counter. Mary Rose took a magazine over to Robbie and pointed to the young woman on the front, "Impossible body construction," she whispered.

"Ya think?" Robbie said and smiled.
Shortly after 12:30 a man walked over from the truck stop and came into the shop. He saw the four ladies and stopped. They

smiled at him. He moved slowly over to the magazine rack and Mary Rose moved over beside him.

He picked up a magazine.

She clasped her hands demurely behind her back and peered over his shoulder.

He put it back and moved over to the videos. Robbie moved over, too.

"Do you want something, lady?" he asked.

Robbie smiled and shook her head, looking right into his eyes.

"Damn," he whispered, and left the store.

"You can't do that!" Lionel said.

"Do what, dear?" Hadley said.

"You scared him off!"

"What's to be scared of?"

In the next two hours, three other customers left without a purchase. Maggie picked up a bookmark shaped like over-sized breasts and took it to the counter.

"I want to purchase this, please," she said, and fluttered what little eyelashes she had left at Lionel.

"Shit," he mumbled under his breath as he rang up her purchase.

"Okay," Lionel said after another half hour had passed, "what the hell are you four old biddies doing in my shop?"

"He called us biddies," Mary Rose said.

"He called us old," Robbie said.

"Reprehensible," Hadley said.

"I don't like his attitude," Maggie said. She smiled a mean little smile. "We're here to put you out of business, Mr. Starkbetter. We're your worst nightmare."

"That's a terrible line, Maggie," Hadley said, "however, she's correct. We represent a young lady named Polly Panchero and until you agree to stop threatening and harassing her we will be here every day greeting your customers."

Lionel snorted.

"I figured you were either a bunch of right-wing religious bitches or those weirdo feminist bitches who think I degrade women."

"He called us bitches," Mary Rose said,.

"He called us weirdos," Robbie said.

"Plus," Maggie said, "we know you're dealing drugs from behind that dirty curtain."

They stared at her, then Lionel snorted again and walked off to the cash register.

"We don't know that!" Robbie whispered.

"We do now," Maggie said and pointed at the curtain where Lionel was hurrying to get out of sight.

Hadley and Mary Rose stayed while the other two went for a coffee break in mid-afternoon. When they came back, Mary Rose wanted to go to the trailer and take Edith Ann out. Hadley volunteered to drive her and said she would make a quick trip to visit the local law enforcement.

"I think it would be wise to tell them what we're doing and let them know about Starkbetter threatening Polly," she said.

She dropped Mary Rose off and played with the Global Positioning System in the Hummer. It showed her the nearest police office was not the police, but the country sheriff. "We had good luck with the last sheriff," she said to the Hummer, "maybe we're on a roll." And she let the GPS lead her two miles down the road to a county building with two sheriff's cruisers and a small Ford parked out front. She parked next to one cruiser, got out and went inside.

The interior of the cinder block building was clean and attractive. A woman in her mid fifties sat behind a counter in a reception area. She smiled at Hadley.

"I'd like to see the sheriff," Hadley smiled back.

"He's in," the receptionist said, and she pointed to an open door behind and to the right of the counter. Hadley walked through the door and stopped.

Standing up to greet her was the most handsome Native American man she had ever seen. She sucked in a breath and her stomach at the same time. The sheriff walked toward her and held out his hand. "Hello. I'm Wes Longbow. How can I help you?"

Wes Longbow was six two and built like a set of truck tires that worked out every day. He wore the same brown uniform that Parker Roberts wore and had a small gold eagle on a chain around his neck. His hair was short and grey and he had a well-groomed mustache. Hadley had an image of him arresting women by just standing in front of them until they fell into his arms in a dead faint. She stared at him.

"M'am?" he finally said.

Hadley shook her head. "Oh. I'm sorry. My head went somewhere else, I guess." She held out her hand, "Hadley Morris-Winfield from Nebraska."

He motioned her toward a comfortable chair in front of his desk and sat beside her in the matching one. His office was unique. The desk was a large antique walnut, on one wall hung an antique regulator clock that was ticking away the minutes. A gun rack filled with rifles hung next to it. Another wall was filled with large framed Tom Mangelsen photographs of polar bears. Hadley had one in her apartment at Meadow Lakes. On the third wall were hung priceless Navajo rugs tastefully displayed. On the wall behind her, Hadley had noticed framed certificates and photographs of the sheriff with various officials and one of him in a San Francisco 49er's uniform, on one knee with his helmet in his hands. She turned and pointed to it. "You were a pro?"

"Offensive tackle until I blew a knee," he smiled at her.

*Be still my heart!*

"How offensive were you?" she asked.

He grinned a beautiful grin, "Very," he said.

*Oh my God, I'm flirting with him.*

She got down to business. "Do you know a man named Lionel Starkbetter?":

"Good old Lionel. I've made his acquaintance numerous times. Got him once on possession and once for dealing. Petty stuff. "

"Have you ever met a nice young woman named Polly Panchero?"

"Hey Miss," the sheriff nodded, "know her from the truck stop."

Hadley told him what was going on, eliminating Polly's tuition financing program. She told him what they were doing at the Adult Emporium. Wes threw his head back and laughed. He smiled a melting smile at Hadley and said quietly, "There's a little cafeteria here in the county building. You have time for a cup of coffee?"

"I do," she said, and thought to herself, *Forgive me Mary Rose. I'm going to be late.*

Mary Rose was watching for her and scurried out the door when the Hummer pulled up beside the trailer. "Where have you been? I started to worry."

"Covering our biddie-bitch asses," Hadley said, and she told her about her meeting with Wes Longbow.

They walked into the emporium just as Maggie pulled out a badge, showed it to a grimy-looking customer and said, "Agent Patten here. Do you have any knowledge about the drugs being sold in this establishment?" The man turned and hurried out the door. Lionel was somewhere behind the curtain.

"Maggie!" Hadley said, "what are you doing? Where did you get that badge?"

"Dollar store next door. Comes with its own case." And she showed them a child's toy FBI badge in a cheap black wallet."

"I wish I'd thought of that," Mary Rose said. "I always wanted to say something like that."

Hadley told Robbie and Maggie about her visit to the real local law. "He'll be here at five o'clock."

At one minute before five, the sheriff's cruiser pulled in and parked directly in front of the store. Wes Longbow stuck his long legs out of the driver's side, got out and ambled up to the door.

*First class ambling*, Hadley thought.

The bell on the door rang as Wes entered and Lionel came out from behind the curtain. "Oh crap," he said.

"And it's good to see you too, Lionel."

Lionel's face brightened. "Actually, I'm glad you're here, Sheriff. I want to lodge a complaint against these four women here. They've been loitering on my premises."

"Did they cause any distraction?"

"They chased away customers! That's what they did?"

"Physically chased? As in run after and threaten bodily harm?"

"No but..."

"Did they use foul language or make verbal threats?"

"No but..."

"Did they make any purchases?"

Maggie held up her bookmark and smiled. Lionel glared at her.

"Lionel, I know what these ladies are doing and we're all going to see you don't bother little Hey Miss any more. The ladies are going to leave now, but I have some paperwork to do, so I'll be parked right outside at your door working with my computer. In a couple of hours one of my deputies will have paperwork to do, then another deputy is going to get caught up, so someone from my office will be outside until you close."

"You can't do that!" Lionel sputtered. "Nobody will come in if that cruiser is parked out front! And it's illegally parked, by Gawd! It's not inside the white lines, it's parallel like you're making an arrest or something." He looked at the women. "This is a conspiracy!"

"No dear," Hadley said. "A conspiracy is when a group plans in devious ways to oust, overcome or defeat another person or group," She thought for a second. "You're right. It's a conspiracy."

Wes smiled, touched his hat and nodded at the BOOB girls. "Ladies, enjoy your evening." And he held the door open for them.

They ate at the truck stop and were served by Polly.

"Whatcha been doing all day, girls?"

"Looking at books mostly," Robbie said.

"That's nice. Bet you had a relaxing time," and she patted Robbie affectionately on the shoulder.

They ate in silence until Mary Rose asked Maggie, "What time does that dollar store open? I have an idea."

The next day when Lionel opened the adult emporium he saw the four women, all dressed in black, leaning against their black Hummer, their arms crossed, glaring at him.

"Charlie's Angels escaped from the nursing home," he mumbled to himself.

Hadley was in her black pantsuit, Mary Rose was dressed in black pants with a black shirt and black vest, Robbie had on a black turtleneck and black pants. Maggie however, was in black fatigues, black boots and a black hat with FBI in white letters across the front.

"Where did you get all that?" Hadley asked.

"Goodwill army surplus," and Maggie started to swagger across the parking lot toward the shop. The others swaggered after her.

In their pockets were toy badges in their cheap cases, purchased when the dollar store opened. This morning they didn't follow Lionel inside. Instead they marched lock-step, side-by-side toward the shop. "I can hear the theme from *Rocky* playing in my head," Mary Rose said. They stood in front of the store, side-by-side again, arms crossed. Lionel peered at them through the window.

Nothing happened for half an hour. No one moved. "I think my ankles are starting to swell," Mary Rose said.

Finally a customer pulled up. All four women moved toward him. He was a young man in jeans and a Dallas Cowboys sweatshirt and cap and worn high top shoes. He paused with the door of his jeep still open. "Yeah?" he said.

Robbie walked closer and flashed her badge at him. "We're investigating drug dealing taking place in this store," she nodded toward the emporium. "Do you mind if we search your vehicle before you go in and again when you return?"

Maggie had pulled out a pad and pen, also from the dollar store, and was writing down his license plate number.

"Jeesuz officers," he said, "I'm on parole. You're not tagging me for this!" and he jumped back in the jeep and peeled out of the parking lot, barely missing Maggie who jumped out of the way from behind the jeep.

"I get to say it next," Mary Rose said.

There had been only four customers, one a young woman who had been in the store the day before and had gone behind the curtain with Lionel and come out after only five minutes. She had a full sleeve of multiple heart tattoos. "Muddy's kinda girl," Maggie said. "She's the drug connection, bet your sweet boobies." They let her go inside without a word.

Wes sent a deputy to check on them mid-afternoon. They didn't mention the badges or say why they were in the parking lot instead of inside the store. He was young and polite and called them all 'M'am' when he spoke and each time he spoke he touched the brim of his hat. It looked as if he didn't yet need to shave.

"Sweet," Robbie said when he left, "he'll be a good cop when he graduates from high school."

"When they're that young," Hadley said, "I always

want to call them 'son' and pat their little heads."

Around 4pm a big Cadillac pulled up in front of the store. An elderly gentleman in an expensive suit got out.

"Drug lord," Maggie said. They walked toward him, just a little apprehensive. He stopped, smiled and listened while they gave their search your car speech. He smiled some more.

"Okay, you're too old to be officers, I know – I'm retired from a state attorney general's office. What are you really doing here?"

They looked at each other, and then they all looked at Hadley. She took at deep breath.

"There's this young woman who works at the truck stop," she began, and she told him the whole story.

"Hey Miss," he said. "She just waited on me. I was headed toward the dollar store down the way. I try to park a ways away from where I'm going so I can limber up my knees." He bent and rubbed his right knee. "The dollar stores usually have an old hand soap that's hard to find and I stop whenever I run across one." He smiled again. "But I can make a quick stop in here," he nodded toward Lionel who was still watching from the window.

The gentleman walked slowly toward the shop. They heard the bell ring as he opened the door. They all moved closer so they could see through the dirty window.

The man in the suit was talking rapidly to Lionel, pointing toward the parking lot then toward the truck stop then punching his finger into Lionel's chest. Lionel was waving his arms and shaking his head. The man pulled out his wallet and showed something to Lionel, who waved and shook harder. Then the gentleman grabbed Lionel by the front of his shirt and yelled something into his face.

"Bet he got some spit and spray with that one," Maggie said.

A few minutes more of yelling and waving and they saw Lionel hurry behind his curtain and the gentleman walked out of the store. "Nice meeting you ladies," he said and nodded at them. "Need anything from the dollar store?"

Wes came by promptly at five again. "Tomorrow I'm going to put some pressure on our friend Lionel," he said, "You four can take a day off."

It was a relief to be off their feet for awhile. They read, cleaned, walked Edith Ann, who was especially glad to have them home again, and Robbie searched for and found a five-day cruise along the coast with one stop in southern California. It left in eight days. It was perfect.

The next morning there was a gentle rain and the girls decided to spend the day inside with Lionel. Around nine o'clock Polly knocked on their door. "There's a fire down by the truck stop," she said. "I heard it on the radio. Let's go see what it is." Edith Ann jumped into her arms and they all squeezed into the Hummer. Robbie drove.

When they got near the truck stop they could see the XXX- Girls sign crumbling to the pavement. The entire building was on fire with flames shooting out of the roof. The bags of garbage near the friendly neighborhood dumpster were giving off an interesting odor of burned food and smoldering diapers. Wes Longbow's cruiser was parked near two fire trucks. Fire fighters were shooting water from four different hoses. A crowd had gathered from the truck stop, watching the action. Robbie parked well back in the parking lot. Wes saw them and ambled over.

Amble on, cowboy, amble on. Hadley stepped forward to greet him. He nodded and touched his hat brim.

"I think you may have succeeded more than you intended to," he smiled. "The fire chief is ninety-nine percent sure this is arson. I have an arrest warrant out for Lionel, but he's no where to be found right now."

"Arson," Hadley whispered. She looked toward Polly, then back at the sheriff. "She doesn't know anything about this." He nodded, leaned against the Hummer and folded his arms.

"I think Lionel may show up," he said, "lots of times this type of thing is spontaneous combustion caused by the insurance policy rubbing up against the mortgage." He smiled again. Lionel may try to collect on the insurance. He owned the building. Other than for the dollar store, it's a good example of necessary urban renewal." There was a pause. He looked at Hadley. "You want to have dinner with me tonight? We could celebrate. I know a nice restaurant about thirty miles from here. Nice venue, good food, great atmosphere."

"I'd love that," she smiled back. *Be still my heart again!*

# Some Enchanted Evening – and Morning – and Afternoon

Hadley was pacing back and forth in the trailer, her arms held straight out in the air. "I'm sweating! I am SO nervous. You'd think I was some brain-dead teenager on a first date!"

The other girls were sitting on the couch and in a recliner, their legs tucked under them to give her room. Edith Ann was hiding in a secure place under the table, her head moving back and forth with Hadley's pacing.

Hadley had spent forty five minutes choosing between the only three outfits she thought suitable. There was not a lot of closet space in a trailer when four women shared it. She had chosen a long black skirt, a grey turtleneck and the black jacket that went with both skirt and pantsuit. She had on two inch black heels and wore pearl earrings and a matching necklace. She had taken a good half hour with her makeup and another twenty minutes with her hair.

"You look good Babe," Robbie encouraged.

At five minutes before six Wes pulled up in a gleaming red Jeep Grand Cherokee.

"Jeep man," Maggie said, "my kinda guy."

He got out and started toward the trailer.

"Don't get pregnant," Maggie smiled.

"Use protection," Robbie said.

"Safe sex is in, but abstinence means no sin," Mary Rose said and they all started to giggle.

"Shhhhhh!" Hadley said, and she grabbed her black purse and hurried out the door. They all tumbled out after her.

"Oh geez," Hadley said.

"Hey Wes," Maggie said.

"Yo WesMan," Robbie said.

"Howdy Sheriff," Mary Rose said.

*Howdy Sheriff???* Hadley thought.

"Ladies," Wes said. He was grinning wider than the three standing before him. The girls were settled in for a relaxing evening and were wearing their pajamas, nightgowns and robes with flip-flops on their feet. Maggie had on only her red long johns.

"You two kids have fun now," Robbie said.

"Don't be late," Mary Rose said.

"Sock it to her," Maggie grinned.

Wes grinned wider and opened the passenger side door for Hadley, who gave the cheerleaders a little finger wave then just gave them the finger. They all waved back as the jeep started down the road out of the campground.

"Popcorn and a movie?" Robbie asked.

"Should we wait up for her?" Mary Rose asked.

"Get a life girl," Maggie said. And she swatted Mary Rose on the rear and made a quick, obscene movement with her hips.


Hadley and Wes showed up at the trailer just before noon the next day. Wes was carrying a large pizza and Hadley had an eight-pack of diet 7up.

"Nice evening?" Maggie asked her.

"Very nice, thank you."

"Have fun?" Robbie asked.

"Lots, thank you."

"Were you good?" Mary Rose asked.

"She was outstanding!" Wes answered and plopped the pizza down on the table. Hadley began breaking out ice cubes and filling glasses with ice and soda.

They sat around the living room eating pizza off of paper towels, giving Edith Ann tiny bites and laughing. Wes told how his father was an actual Indian chief, a Kiowa who moved to the west coast because his mother was a Methodist missionary and insisted on naming him John Wesley after the founder of the faith. "I'm more a flounderer of the faith now," he said. Mary Rose announced she was a recovering Catholic. Robbie said she and her husband had attended a big church on their campus. "Prayer hung heavy on the walls. It was nice," she said. Hadley admitted to being a stereotype Episcopalian. Maggie admitted to being nothing at all.

About an hour into the conversation Hadley reached over and took hold of Maggie's hand. "Maggie, we did something without asking you. Wes and I drove down to the city and did a search for your boy Harley."

"Hadley told me the story, Maggie," Wes said. "We went to the FBI office and police headquarters. The long and short of it is, we couldn't find Harley Patten anywhere." Maggie squeezed Hadley's hand. "Thanks," she said. "I thought about asking you to see what you could find on the coast here, but I guess I was afraid you'd either find out he was dead or find out he was alive and either way I'd have to figure out what the hell to do." She smiled at them. "But thanks again. I appreciate it."

"It's not the end of the story," Wes went on. "We found that about fifteen years ago a sizable group of gay men in the San Francisco area organized a medical group and went to Africa. We think Harley may have been part of those volunteers."

"That would be like him," Maggie said. She thought for a minute. "Gawd. He'd be fifty-five now." She smiled. "He's old enough to have a damn AARP card."

"You know you're old when your children have AARP cards," Robbie said. "Maybe next year we could plan a trip to Africa. We are adventurin' wimmen."

Maggie smiled at them, tears glistening in her eyes.

## Pity-pat, Pity-pat, Boom, Boom, Boom

The cruise was three days away. Maggie was looking over the brochures Robbie had ordered and Mary Rose was making a careful list of what they should take with them on the ship. Polly had been excited when they asked her to keep Edith Ann and had even taken her to work one shift. She came home even more excited. "The girls in the office love her!" she said. "She can come to work with me and stay in there with them anytime I want to bring her.

"You realize this is for senior citizens?" Maggie asked, waving the brochure.

"Duh," Robbie said. "What do you think we are girlfriend?"

Hadley picked up another brochure and spread it

open. "Yeah, but look at this, one of the shows features the Chippendales."

"You're kidding me!" Maggie said, grabbing for the brochure.

Hadley held it above her head. "I am, but the fantasy is worth having."

They were excited. Hadley had been on two cruises with her husband, Robbie had been to Europe but had flown and neither Maggie nor Mary Rose had ever been on a big ship in big water. "Better pack Dramamine just in case," Mary Rose had said and wrote it on her list.

At 2am the following morning Maggie shook Hadley and Mary Rose awake. "Robbie's heart went out of rhythm. We need to get her to a hospital right away. Hurry up." Her voice was hoarse with anxiety. They rushed to get dressed. Robbie was waiting in the living room, wearing a jogging suit and holding the stuffed black bear she had brought with her and kept on her bed. She looked grey and her face was wet with sweat. She leaned against the back of the couch and took deep breaths. When Hadley walked over and put her hand on her forehead, Robbie felt cold and clammy. "Sorry guys," she whispered.

The GPS in the Hummer gave them turn-by-turn directions to the nearest hospital ten miles away. They parked in front of the emergency room entrance and Hadley took one of Robbie's hands and walked with her inside. She clutched the little bear close to her chest. Maggie walked on the other side of Robbie, close to her.

They were still sitting at an admitting station when Mary Rose came in from parking the Hummer. The tired lady behind the desk had made copies of Robbie's Medicare card and supplemental insurance card. There had been a computer glitch that slowed her down. Robbie's heart was racing so fast Hadley couldn't count the beats where she was holding Robbie's left wrist.

"What does this usually get up to?" she asked with a note of fear in her voice.

"It can get up close to 200 a minute," Robbie breathed. "Some people go as high as 300, and then it's really dangerous."

"Can you hurry please," Hadley said to the receptionist. A nurse appeared with a wheelchair and they all followed the nurse and Robbie into the treatment area. In just minutes Robbie was in a hospital gown, hooked up to a monitor that read her heartbeat and blood pressure. An oxygen tube was in her nose. A young doctor appeared and looked at the monitor and asked Robbie questions. The other three stood to one side and their body language made it clear they weren't going to leave. They heard him say, "electo-cardioversion" and Robbie nodded and held up three fingers.

A cart was rolled in and another nurse appeared. "I'm your nurse anesthetist," she said. "Ready for sleepy time?" She inserted an IV into Robbie's vein. The doctor pulled the cart up close to Robbie and held two paddles up. The nurse anesthetist threaded a shot of anesthesia into the IV.

"I always ask if I can have some of this to go," Robbie smiled. "It's gr...." and she was out. The doctor placed the paddles on Robbie's chest and even though the other three did their best to see what was happening, they couldn't see past the doctor's back. But they did hear the monitor slow down and see Robbie's heartbeat return to normal. They all blew out their breaths in relief.

"She'll be awake in a few minutes and I'll be back then and we'll talk." He left. They looked at each other. They moved over and surrounded Robbie who was sleeping like a baby and still clutching the bear. Hadley lifted it out of her arms and cuddled it. There was a tiny button on each forepaw. Hadley pressed one.

"My sweet girl," a croaking old lady's voice came through a hidden recording, "I am so proud of you. You have been more than I could ever have dreamt and I love you more than you could ever dream."

"It's her mother," Mary Rose whispered. Hadley pressed the other paw.

"Hey Chocolate," a man's voice said, "you're my baby forever and I cannot imagine life without you. Thank you for being my wife. I love you, I love you, I love you." The tape ended with a soft, romantic laugh.

"It's her husband," Maggie whispered. "He called her Chocolate. That's why she got so mad at the jerk at the Ragged Ass." They passed the little bear around and each gave it a hug.

"Be all right, Robbie, be all right," Mary Rose whispered. Just then the doctor came back.

"I want to keep her overnight, just in case," he said. "Are you family?" They looked at each other.

"Sisters," Hadley said then paused for just a second, "different fathers." The doctor raised one eyebrow and looked at each of them. Robbie opened her eyes. The doctor moved toward her.

"I want you overnight – maybe two nights – to run some tests and get a cardiologist on board here."

"I can't stay over," Robbie said, her voice almost a whine, "we have a cruise day after tomorrow." The doctor just smiled and walked out. In just a minute a large, motherly nurse walked in.

"We have a room ready for you, and no arguments, honey. You're more important than a cruise and we're going to take good care of you. Now you be good and we'll get this all fixed up. Someone will take you to your room in just a minute." And she turned around and walked back out.

"She's patronizing me!" Robbie said. She glared after the nurse then looked at her three friends. "I've had all the tests. I know what's going on. I will not stay here and miss the cruise of my life!" and she began to cry.

All three moved in and hugged her. There was a long silence.

"You sure, Robbie?" Hadley asked. Robbie gave a very definite nod yes. Hadley thought for a minute while the others looked from her to Robbie and back again.

Then Hadley smiled. "I used to volunteer at the hospital. I have an idea. Let them take you up, Robbie. We'll be up later. We're going to spring you."

"I love police talk," Mary Rose said. "How do we spring her?"

"Follow me," Hadley said, and they walked out of the draped ER treatment room just as a transport cart came to take Robbie upstairs.

Hadley led them to the nearest elevator, pushed the down button and when they were inside, pushed B for basement.

In the pre-dawn hours, the basement hallways were lit with dim, eerie lighting that cast a yellow spell over the ceiling and walls. The floors were grey tile with a yellow line down the center. "Don't tell me we're headed for the morgue," Maggie said.

"Look for a room marked either 'uniforms' or 'supplies,'" Hadley said. They crept along like two-bit criminals. Finally, after turning two corners they came to 'linen supplies' on a door. Hadley nodded toward it, then moved forward and tried the knob. It was open.

Five minutes later, three doctors emerged in white coats, their hair in surgery caps. None had stethoscopes around her neck. None had a name written on the pocket of her coat. All had a determined look and one, the shortest, carried a fourth white coat over her arm.

"What now, doctor?" Mary Rose whispered.

"We find the cardiology floor," Hadley whispered back.

They walked boldly into the deserted lobby and looked at the big directory inside the front doors. 'Cardiology 7th floor' it read. "Big place," Maggie said. They once again grabbed the nearest elevator. A nurse got off when the door opened but never glanced at them.

Hadley looked at her watch. "The 7am shift will be here any time. That's when we get out of here."

The hallway on seven was deserted except for one nurse who was walking toward the elevator. Immediately the three doctors bent their heads together in an obviously serious consultation, motioning with their hands, nodding and theorizing. The nurse disappeared into a room down the hall without looking their way.

There was no one at the nurses' station. "How do we find her?" Maggie asked.

"Look in every room?" Mary Rose said.

Just then an orderly came out of a room on the other side of the nurses' station pushing the transport cart.

"Thank you, Jesus!" Mary Rose said and they hurried as fast as they could to door left open by the orderly. Robbie was sitting up in bed, holding her bear. When she saw the three girls she broke into a huge smile. "Hello doctors," she said.

"Here's the plan," Hadley said. "Robbie, you put on the other coat and cap. You're going to have to take it slow going to the truck, so Maggie will lie down on the bed and we'll transfer all those cute little white buttons that are monitoring your heart to Maggie. Mary Rose can go bring the Hummer around." She walked over and looked out the window. "Good. There's an entrance right below us. Mary Rose, come look." Mary Rose looked, found landmarks and went to get the Hummer.

"Maggie," after you're rigged up, give us fifteen minutes to get Robbie dressed and to the Hummer, then run like the wind out of here," Hadley said.

"That will be something to see," Maggie said. She lay down beside Robbie and Hadley and Mary Rose began removing the body monitors from Robbie and transferring them to Maggie's chest. Twice the machine sent out an emergency signal but quieted right away. Each time, all four women held their breath and watched the door.

"Hate to say it, Maggie, but you're normal," Robbie said as she watched Maggie's heart take over the monitor. Robbie slipped into her jogging suit, put on the white coat and nodded to Hadley.

The three white coats walked slowly out the door and down the hall. The shift was changing and nurses were clustered around the nurses' station. The doctors turned a corner some distance from the station and went to a second bank of elevators. Robbie herself pushed the down button. Three visitors exited the elevator and nodded to the doctors who nodded back. The elevator stopped on the third floor and the girls held their breaths, but no one got on. At ground floor level they strolled slowly through the lobby, went through the big doors and Hadley pointed to the Hummer waiting a short distance away. Robbie sighed, shifted her little bear to the other arm and began to walk.

"Hadley, where's that other entrance? I don't see the landmarks I noticed from the room on seven," Mary Rose asked from behind the wheel as Robbie slid into the back seat and pulled off the surgery cap, Mary Rose had thrown her white coat and cap into the back seat and Hadley took hers off as she got in.

"Entrance is right beside here," Hadley said, motioning to the nearby wall. They pulled around to a side entrance near the main doors. Hadley gathered the white coats and began to fold them. When she was done she got out and carefully carried them to a spot near the main entrance, laid them on the sidewalk and hurried back. They waited.

"It's been twenty minutes," Mary Rose said. "How are you feeling, Robbie?"

"I'm good," Robbie answered. They waited another five minutes.

"What should we do?" Hadley asked.

"I can go look for her," Mary Rose said. "I look the most innocent."

Just then Maggie came running full speed from the front of the building, her little bow legs pumping, her arms flying. She dived into the back seat. She was wearing her street clothes and breathing hard. "Couldn't find the damn entrance!" she gasped. Mary Rose stepped on the gas and they drove out of the parking lot as if it was the most normal thing in the world to do.

*The only good thing about wrinkles is they don't hurt.*

## PART FOUR:

# Riding the Long Freight Home*

*I do not fear death*
*Oh God, it is the dying.*

*Robert James Waller, Border Music

# Cruising Big Time

They left the Hummer in the garage owned by the cruise line and pulled their carry-on bags up the ramp to the monster ship decked out in banners and flags. Robbie was feeling fine but they were taking no chances. Mary Rose pulled Robbie's suitcase along with her own. "They have defibrillators on board a cruise ship!" Robbie insisted. "We don't care," Mary Rose had said, and grabbed ahold of the handle.

They were welcomed with champagne (soda for Robbie) and cake. Their stateroom was on a lower deck, but was elegant and comfortable. The four single beds were covered with thick comforters. Maggie grabbed hers, wrapped it around her shoulders and said, "Ain't nothin' better than this, girls. Ain't nothin' better," and she flopped down on the couch beneath the port hole.

They watched standing on their deck as the big ship took to sea, then they began to explore. They found the dining room they liked best. They found the casino and the dance floor and the library and the game room. But best of all, they found the deck. Wrapped in the comforters from their beds, they watched the stars come our after a lavish dinner and talked. As usual they spoke of more than shoes and ships and sealing wax, of cabbages and kings.

"I always thought the sea was romantic," Mary Rose said. "I loved the Pirates of the Caribbean movies."

"What's not to love with Johnny Depp in it," Robbie said.

"Those old, old pirate movies with burials at sea were romantic, too," Hadley added.

"I'll be buried by my husband," Mary Rose said. "He probably won't recognize me now that I don't look dowdy any more."

A steward brought them cups of steaming hot chocolate.

"The life!" Maggie said and cupped hers in her hands.

"I'll be buried by my guy, too," Robbie said.

"I'll be in an urn by whatever is in the urn next to me," Hadley said and laughed a soft laugh.

"I want to be buried here," Maggie said after a short silence.

"You can't be buried here, girlfriend," Hadley said, "we're on the water."

"I know that! I want a burial at sea."

They looked at her and smiled. Robbie did a small eye roll.

"I mean it, you turkeys!" Maggie said. "I love it here. I think we should be like that lady on the Queen Elizabeth who lived on the ship full time. I never knew about the ocean so I never missed it, but I am at home here. I love it!"

"Home is the sailor – home from the sea," Robbie quoted, "but you're the sailor home on the sea."

"It is nice," Mary Rose said.

"I'm serious, girls," Maggie went on. "I don't want to be buried by my sonuvabitch husband. My name isn't on that tombstone. Homer is probably scattered to the four winds in the Sand Hills now. I have no place to go, no one to visit my grave. When I die, whoever of you three is left, I want you to somehow get me back to the ocean and give me a burial at sea, and not just my ashes. I want a real body burial, wrapped up nice and my whole self dumped into that water. The best fish food ever. Period. I will swim with the sharks and not be afraid."

They were all quiet.

"C'mon, Maggie," Hadley said. "We can't do that. What would we do? How do you arrange something like that?"

"You escaped from a retirement community, howled like wolves, taped a killer, J. Frederick Sapp to his bed, rescued a dog, shut down a porno shop and got tattooed. And you're saying you can't find a way to get a one hundred pound package into the water? Rent a boat for Christ's sake!"

"For Christ's sake would mean you'd have a religious sinking," Mary Rose said and she slapped Maggie's arm and laughed.

The cruise was good to them and for them. The next day they each took fifty dollars to lose in the ship's casino, but Mary Rose hit a jackpot, collected five-hundred dollars and took them all to the ship's boutique and bought them matching rain jackets with the ship logo on the pocket.

"Way cool," Maggie said.

"Way nice," Hadley said.

"Way generous," Robbie said.

"Way welcome," Mary Rose said.

They wore them that evening when they walked the deck. This time their conversation led to talk of dying. "Remember in that *Grumpy Old Men* movie where Jack Lemon and Walter Mathow would hear of someone dying suddenly and they'd say, 'Lucky bastard?'" Robbie said. "I'm hoping with my heart problem that's how I'll go. Quick."

"My family mostly died of cancer," Hadley said. "Not a

great thing. I guess I will just say my four words over and over every day if that comes my way – 'grace, humor, courage and confidence'."

"Mine probably won't be any easier," Mary Rose said. "I have three women relatives who actually died of old age. My grandmother was the meanest woman I ever knew and she lived to be ninety-four. My aunt lived to be over one hundred. My mother was eighty-five and as mean as my grandmother and if she hadn't been hit by a train, she would still be alive."

They looked at her. "Hit by a train?" Robbie asked.

"Tended to take walks on the railroad tracks along the river. Saw a quarter. Bent over to pick it up. Never heard the train. Toot toot, she never came back."

Maggie snorted. "Sorry," she smiled. "But I think that's kinda classy. I want to go with some drama. Having really enthusiast sex would work for me." They all swatted her and laughed.

On the third day of the cruise they docked at a small island off the southern California coast and drank from tall glasses with fruit and topped off with tiny umbrellas. They shopped and bought trinkets. Robbie announced that she felt better than she ever had after a cardioversion. Maggie said that was better than announcing you had regular bowel movements, and they told more jokes and laughed harder than they had in a long time. But it was the last day before the ship returned to port that Mary Rose had the most memorable experience of her life.

# *O! O! O!*

"Hey girls, get a load of this," Maggie said. She was holding a pink sheet of paper that had been slipped beneath their door during the night.

### O! O! O!
*An independent company*
*Presents Dr. Olivia Olivet O'Donnell*
*"Wrinkles Away Forever"*
*Lecture on aging gracefully.*
*A Free sample of Dr. O'Donnell's new,*
*miracle anti-aging cream to every lady attending.*
*Guaranteed to make facial wrinkles disappear.*
*4pm today*
*Main auditorium*
*You won't believe the face you see in the mirror!*

"I don't believe the face I see now in the mirror," Maggie said.

"Are there other wrinkles besides facial ones?" Mary Rose asked.

Hadley held up her arm, pulled up her sleeve and pointed to the underside of her upper arm. "Lots!" she said.

"Free miracle cream," Mary Rose said. "And we have nothing else to do this afternoon."

They went.

The auditorium was nearly full when they walked through the door. Only the front two rows of seats were not occupied. They headed toward the first row and the stage where a short, bald man was pacing and looking at his watch.

"Tad nervous there," Robbie said.

They waited and chatted and looked at their watches almost as often as the nervous man on the stage. An attractive young woman hurried to the stage, bent and whispered something in his ear. He began yelling at her, waving his arms, bending his knees and bobbing up and down.

The young woman looked past his bobbing and waving toward the audience. She looked at Mary Rose, grabbed the man's arm, turned him around and pointed to Mary Rose. He stared. He jabbered to the young woman. She nodded and they turned and walked down the steps from the stage and stood in front of the four friends.

"Excuse me," he said to Mary Rose. All four women stood up. The man was about the same height as Maggie. He was wearing a tuxedo with a white rose in his lapel and beads of sweat stood out on his forehead. He looked remarkably like a weasel.

"I'm Norman Cuzzle, Executive Director of Olivia Olivet O'Donnell's company, O! O! O! and I have a great favor to ask of you which will definitely be to your benefit." Everyone was quiet. The background talk from the audience was getting louder as time was passing. They were definitely behind schedule now.

"You see," Norman Cuzzle began, "Dr. O'Donnell is unable to join us. We have a small prepared speech and we would like you," he pointed to Mary Rose, "to just go to the podium, read the speech and sit down. We'll give you a full six-month supply of miracle wrinkle remover." He hesitated.

"Not that you need it, dear lady, not that you need it." Maggie touched his arm. "Just exactly why isn't the good doctor herself here?" she asked.

"There's been an unfortunate incident," he said.

"She's passed out dead drunk in her room," the young woman standing beside him said with a grim, vengeful smile. She was a good six inches taller than Cuzzle and was wearing a very tasteful red Chanel suit and three-inch heels. Her mass of curls took on a life of their own. All four women smiled at her. She smiled back and did an eye roll toward Norman Cuzzle.

Mary Rose stood as tall as possible and looked down at Cuzzle. "You want me to impersonate a doctor, read a speech without telling them who I really am and all I'm getting is a big jar of useless cream? I don't think so."

Norman Cuzzle stammered and bobbed again. "I'll give you two hundred dollars," he sputtered.

Mary Rose paused. The crowd noise came through loud and clear. "These," she said motioning to Hadley, Robbie and Maggie, "are my esteemed colleagues. There are four of us. That would be a total of eight hundred dollars."

Hadley, Robbie and Maggie dropped their jaws and stared at Mary Rose. Norman Cuzzle bobbed harder and began to wave his arms. The young woman behind him smiled wider. "I can't do that!" he said.

"Then find somebody else," Mary Rose said, and she sat down. Hadley, Robbie and Maggie sat with her.

"But you look exactly like her!" Cuzzle said.

*That explains everything*, Hadley thought.

"Eight hundred cash," Mary Rose said.

Cuzzle sweat harder, then he stopped bobbing and turned to the young assistant. He whispered something in her ear while standing on his tip toes. She walked to the stage, pulled a briefcase from behind the podium, opened it on her knee and returned with a red plastic bank envelope which she handed to Cuzzle.

He opened the envelope and the girls saw it was packed tight with one hundred dollar bills. He counted out eight, handed them to Mary Rose, grabbed her arm and began pulling her onto the stage. Mary Rose pushed the bills to Hadley who reached out and grabbed them just in time.

"Should have asked for more," Maggie said.

Cuzzle hurried to the podium and turned on the microphone.

"I am so sorry for the delay," he said with a broad smile. "Now she is here and she is ready. Ladies please welcome Dr. Olivia Olivet O'Donnell, the scientist who founded O! O! O!, the company that discovered the miracle wrinkle cream that proudly carries the name itself," and he actually struck a cheerleader pose, raised one arm yelled, "O! O! O!" He pushed Mary Rose toward the podium and pointed to a single sheet of paper with two paragraphs written on it. There was polite applause.

"Ladies," Mary Rose began to read, "I thank you for your warm welcome. Who among us on this senior cruise has not wanted to have the smooth skin and beautiful complexion of a teenager?" Mary Rose stopped reading aloud but kept her head down and her lips moving, slowly reading the next few sentences in front of her. The crowd had gone silent.

"Oh to hell with that!" she said loudly. "Who are we kidding? None of us here is ever going to look like a teenager again, and if we do it's because we've just gotten the facelift from hell." There was some scattered laughter. Hadley, Robbie and Maggie looked at each other and shrugged.

"The other day I was watching one of the morning shows, and the hostess, who had probably had a facelift at age thirty (snickers from the audience) announced that after the break we would hear about new make-up and fashions for the older woman in her forties. Give me a break! Older women in their forties? Women in their forties are babies. Women in their fifties are babies. Show me the woman in her sixties, her seventies, her eighties and nineties and I'll show you a WOMAN!"

There was louder scattered applause from the audience. Mary Rose's three friends were sitting, mouths gaping, bug eyed, watching and listening.

"Where?" she asked, "Just where are the models on television and in print who are real women and not anorexic sticks? Where is the make-up just for us? We live in a culture of ageism that is good to men and cruel to women. Why should Sean Connery look terrific just as he is and a beautiful actress the same age be labeled old and out of work?"

There was more applause.

"I say to you," Mary Rose took a deep breath, "we've had enough. If you are a bountiful woman, be proud! If you are ample, be proud. If Queen Latifah loses another pound I'm writing a letter of complaint." (More applause and laughter). "Girls, throw your weight around! There is more woman to the big woman, am I right?"

This time the room went wild with cheers and applause. Robbie leaned over to Hadley and shouted over the crowd noise, "This from a woman who has lost sixty pounds and has more skin than she'll ever use."

Mary Rose McGill was on a roll. "How about fashion

just for us. Look at the women's sections of department stores. Pitiful! While I and my colleagues here," she motioned to her three friends, "while we say at our age we won't wear anything that doesn't feel as comfortable as a bathrobe, we damn well want that comfort to be stylish and we want to be recognized wearing our slacks, our suits, our dresses."

She paused for a drink of water from the glass on the podium. Then she pulled the microphone out of the holder and walked toward the audience.

"Remember the song from *West Side Story*? I Feel Pretty. I don't remember all the words, but join in with what you remember. "I feel pretty," the auditorium filled with voices. "She can't sing!" Maggie said, and she began to sing, too. I feel pretty and witty and bright and I pity, any girl who isn't me tonight." The audience was actually getting into harmony. "Who's that pretty girl in the mirror there? Who can that pretty girl be?" Mary Rose stopped singing and held up her hand. Instant silence.

"That pretty girl is YOU!" she said into the microphone. "That pretty girl is YOU! THAT PRETTY GIRL IS YOU!" The crowd was on its feet applauding. Mary Rose motioned for everyone to sit down. They sat.

"Dress like you want! Be stylish! Wear great make-up. Have your hair done in a style that says 'classy bitch', keep your shoulders straight, your head high, your eyes straight ahead and your tummy tucked in."

"SHIT!" Hadley, Robbie and Maggie yelled together, then quickly covered their mouths with their hands. The crowd laughed.

"My friends and colleagues call ourselves the BOOB girls. It stands for Burned Out Old Broads. But inside we feel twenty five. Inside we feel real and adventurous and glamorous. We're not burned out emotionally, or spiritually. Oh, a whole lot of us are burned out physically. A lot of us here have had hysterectomies, we're wombless wonders. A lot of us are one-breasted or breastless amazons from cancer. Some of us have bags that are not just under our eyes. (Laughter and sounds of agreement). We can't see as well as we could and some of us are stone deaf."

"Sexy people are often hard of hearing," Maggie yelled. Someone across the room yelled, "What?" and the crowd laughed.

Mary Rose smiled and pointed at Maggie. "But our souls are not burned out, no siree! Almost all of us have been hospitalized more than once and we won't even mention those grotesque hospital gowns that demean women of all ages and make us even more vulnerable. I say the next time you have to wear one of those, roll over in bed and moon your doctors and nurses. (Laughter and applause). If you're a large lady, give 'em a FULL moon. (Cheers),

"We're burned out at our society who says we can't think as fast, play as hard or work as well as younger women. Maybe we can't, but we have the wisdom of the ages in our hearts and tolerance and love as well. And we want more for ourselves, more ways to show we're beautiful.

"It's time we had a make-up designer just for us. Let us have make-up that fits our coloring and our faces. Let us be free to choose from a large selection of reasonable and stylish fashion and even larger selection of specialized skin care and make-up. Let us be free to choose and play and have fun with our bodies. Let us be free, free at last, free at last. Praise God Almighty, let us be free at last."

Robbie leaned toward Hadley and Maggie and shouted over the applause, "She just married Martin Luther King Jr. to Estee Lauder."

Mary Rose went to the edge of the stage and sat down, crossing her ankles and looking comfortably at her audience. "What did you see on magazines the last time you were in a supermarket checkout line? You saw anorexic young women and maybe one, handsome older man. Well what if we had our own magazine," she whispered into the microphone. "What if we formed a biddie brigade and all us old biddies wrote to O! O! O!" she suddenly realized who she was supposed to be, "wrote to my company and said we want a magazine for women sixty and over. We want a magazine whose cover features a sixty-year-old one month, a seventy the next, an eighty after that, a ninety-year-old and if a woman reaches one hundred, she's guaranteed a photo shoot with us. This is a magazine, girls, where you have to be carded to buy one. If you're not at least sixty, you're out of luck." (Laughter and applause)

"Think she can get up from there?" Maggie asked Hadley.

Mary Rose twirled around on her butt, put one hand in front of her and rose to her feet in two semi-graceful moves. She held up a tube of the wrinkle cream. "You are beautiful just as you are! This cream is nice. You all have a sample. It was waiting for you on your chairs when you came in. It will soften your skin. It will feel good on your face, but the only way it will make your wrinkles disappear is if you smear it on your mirror. And who wants to get rid of all our wrinkles? You have earned those wrinkles, ladies. You have worked for them! Those wrinkles say you've worn out your worries along with your heartaches. You've fretted over children and husbands and a lot of you here have buried both children and husbands. You've outlived friends and families. How many of you here still have a parent living today?" Two women raised their hands. "That's what I mean," Mary Rose went on. "We've seen it all. We've seen wars and terror and death and grief. We've been misunderstood and underestimated," she paused dramatically.

"Well, let me tell you, this cream says you won't believe the woman you see in the mirror, but it's not because of this cream. You won't believe the woman you see in the mirror when you see yourself as a classy, beautiful, elegant, stylish, brave and courageous old broad." She looked down at her three friends and together they gave her three thumbs up. Then she looked out over the audience. You could have heard a pin drop.

"You are so beautiful," she repeated into the microphone. "You are so very, very beautiful and wise and wonderful. Don't ever think differently. (Dramatic pause) When you look in that mirror I want every one of you to recognize that beauty, that awesomeness that shines through your soul, through your tears and your laughter. Every time you look in that mirror, you say to your heart, 'I am so beautiful', because believe me, you are! You are so beautiful. Don't let anyone ever say you are not. Thank you for letting me be with you today."

Mary Rose McGill bowed her head to her audience and her audience was on their feet, led by none other than Norman Cuzzle who was hopping up and down higher than ever. She handed him the microphone and hurried as fast as she could down the stairs to her three friends while the applause continued. She motioned them to one side and walked down the far aisle of the auditorium to get to the exit before Cuzzle finished his closing remarks which, thanks to Mary Rose, were being very well received.

As soon as the doors opened, the crowd began to pour out. Mary Rose was hurrying ahead so no one could stop her and talk to her. They were in the hallway when they saw a woman who looked remarkably like Mary Rose stagger into the crowd. Her hair looked like a dignified rat's nest, one shoe was missing and her white blouse was partially hanging out from her red suit skirt. "I'm here now!" she was yelling. "You can start!" Hadley turned to see the woman spin around and fall flat on her ample behind. A woman next to her bent to help her up and Hadley heard her say, "Oh you poor dear. Here, take my tube of wrinkle cream, you need it more than I do."

'I think I just saw Olivia Olivet O'Donnell," Hadley said. And she pushed Mary Rose to hurry faster away from the admiring crowd.

# Riding the Long Freight Home*

"Holy Moly," Maggie said when they rushed into their stateroom and locked the door, "where did that come from Mary Rose?"

Mary Rose slumped onto the couch and spread eagle across it. "I have no idea," she said, her voice a little hoarse.

"Fantastic," Hadley said.

"Awesome," Robbie said.

"Holy Moly, "Maggie said again.

They ordered dinner from the steward to be delivered to their stateroom, afraid to face the crowd of women trying for a Mary Rose sighting. "Cuzzle didn't even ask my name," Mary Rose said. "We're safe from him at least."

They couldn't stop talking about what she had done, and finally, just as the stars began to come out Mary Rose looked at Maggie. "I'll risk sitting on deck if we can put on our jackets, pull the hoods up and cover up with the comforters."

"I'm in," Maggie said.

"Not me, I'm finishing a book," Robbie said.

"I'm going to walk around for a few minutes and hear the Mary Rose talk that's going on," Hadley said.

Mary Rose and Maggie snuggled into their recliners on deck. The night was chilly with a brisk wind and a fresh smell of rain to come. "Like I said," Maggie sighed, "don't git no better than this," and she lay back and relaxed in the recliner. Mary Rose followed suit.

An hour passed and a gentle mist began to form. Robbie looked out the port hole. "They'll be running in here any minute," she said to Hadley. "The rain is coming."

In less than three minutes the door flew open. Mary Rose stopped just inside, her face dead white, her hands trembling. "Maggie's dead," she said in a hoarse, whispering voice. "Come right away. Our Maggie's dead."

Hadley grabbed their rain jackets, took hold of Mary Rose's hand and ran behind Robbie. The rain had started and the deck was empty except for the small figure in the recliner, wrapped snuggly in the comforter from her bed. They gathered around her and leaned in.

Maggie was indeed dead. Her eyes and mouth were open and she looked even colder than the rain that was coming down. They stared. Finally Hadley said, "We need to close her eyes." Robbie reached down, put her fingers on Maggie's upper lids and made a downward motion. The lids closed, the mouth stayed open. "Her skin is ice cold." Robbie said.

"Oh my God," Mary Rose said and she began to cry. "What do we do? What do we do?" They were so numb they didn't notice the rain was coming down harder.

"We have to think," Hadley said. "She doesn't have any family, she has nowhere to go, no one but us. I don't even know who to tell."

"She'll end up in the ship's morgue in cold storage and she hates things like that," Mary Rose said.

"She wanted a burial right here," Robbie said.

"That's against the law," Mary Rose added.

They were quiet for a minute.

"So what?" Hadley said. "It was her last wish and she trusted us with it. Even if we get caught and get life in prison what does that mean? Five years? Ten years? Maybe more for you, Mary Rose, since all your women live so long, but it's three hots and a cot and you'll have company."

Mary Rose made a sound between a laugh and a sob.

They were quiet for another two minutes. The rain continued in a steady downpour, running off the hoods of their jackets onto their slacks and shoes, washing the deck in sheets of water.

"We could go inside and plan something," Hadley said, "but I hate to just leave her here."

"So plan here," Robbie said. She thought for a minute. "If we heave her overboard we need to weigh her down."

"I feel like a criminal," Mary Rose said.

"We could tie her suitcase around her," Hadley said, "that would weigh her down and soak up and sink well."

Mary Rose and Robbie nodded.

"Hadley," Robbie said, "we'll stay with Maggie's body. You go pack her suitcase."

Hadley slipped on the wet deck, but made it to the door without falling. Inside she passed another passenger on the way to the elevator. "Dead cold out there," he said. "It certainly is," she answered and she lowered her head and hurried to their stateroom.

She packed all of Maggie's things into her small suitcase, leaving the trinkets she had purchased on the island for the three remaining friends to keep in remembrance. She packed the photo of Harley that Maggie carried with her in a plastic baggie and kept it separate from the suitcase. It would fit in the pocket of her jacket, next to her heart.

Hadley went to her jewelry box and took out the three navel rings Muddy Ink had given them in Resolution. She remembered the surprised look on Jimmy's face and Fat's chuckle when they had pulled up their shirts and shown them off. She put them in the baggie with Harley's picture. Only Maggie had kept her ring in her belly button and now she would take a little bit of their love and laughter with her into the ocean and the next place beyond.

She went through their closets and gathered every belt she could find, then she wheeled the suitcase out the door, gripped the baggie to her heart, held on tight to the belts and leaned into what was now a driving rain.

They unwound the comforter from Maggie's body and tucked it into a corner behind the deck chair. They used the belts to secure the suitcase fast and tight around Maggie's waist. Hadley showed them the photo and the navel rings and they nodded in approval. She zipped the baggie into the inside pocket of Maggie's jacket. The rain was coming down so hard they could barely hear each other.

"Any security cameras on the deck won't be able to see us," Robbie yelled, and she began pushing the chair with Maggie and the suitcase toward the edge of the deck. Hadley pushed with her and Mary Rose pulled.

"Oh crap!" Mary Rose said and she slipped on the wet deck and landed hard on her rear. She got up and began pulling again. Suddenly the chair seemed to take on a life of its own and slid at warp speed to the railing on the deck's edge. They all lost their grip.

Hadley tried to run after it and fell headfirst, banging her head on the wooden deck, "Crap!" she yelled.

Robbie was on her feet, chasing the chair. She slipped and fell flat on her back, "Crap again!" she yelled. The chair acted like a wide receiver headed for the goal line.

Mary Rose made a sliding tackle and captured the chair's leg. Hadley slid to her, braced herself against the railing and the chair stopped. Robbie fell twice before she reached them. "Triple crap," she yelled.

"What now?" Robbie asked.

"We pick the body up, say a few words and throw it into the sea," Hadley said.

"How do you propose we do that?" Mary Rose yelled.

"Grab ahold of the suitcase, Mary Rose," Hadley yelled. "You lift that. Robbie, grab one end of the body and I'll grab the other. On the count of three, we lift and throw. If we could toss J. Frederick Sapp around, we can surely pick up Maggie."

They braced themselves. The rain was coming in torrents now.

"We love you, Maggie," Robbie yelled.

"Thanks for all the adventure," Mary Rose yelled.

"Maggot our Maggot, we will never forget you as long as we live," Hadley yelled.

They were all sobbing, rain washing their tears down their faces.

"One……." They took a deep breath.

"Two……." Hadley yelled as loud as she could. Their faces were set, grim, tear-washed and determined.

"Three!" And together they put every muscle they had into lifting Maggie's body to the top of the railing.

"Push!" Hadley yelled. Lightening was flashing across the horizon and the rain hadn't let up. They were dripping wet and drenched to the bone, but they pushed with all their strength.

The body fell downward toward the one deck lower than theirs.

They listened.

There was no splash.

"Did it go in?" Mary Rose asked.

"Hard to tell with this rain and wind," Robbie said.

"I think we would have heard something that heavy," Hadley said. "It didn't have all that far to go." Their voices were getting hoarse from yelling and they were all getting weaker.

They peered over the deck, holding on tight to the railing. It was too dark and too rainy to see anything.

The next flash of lightning was closer.

"Oh double holy crap," Robbie yelled. Just below them, balancing on the railing, was the body, the suitcase on top of it, swaying in the wind and rolling with the ship as the seas became more violent.

"What do we do if it rolls onto the deck?" Mary Rose yelled.

"We punt," Hadley yelled.

"We're dead meat," Robbie whispered.

Just then a wave rolled against the ship and the lightning flashed again. They leaned over as far as they could without slipping or falling. The ship rocked and as they held their breath, lightning flashed almost directly overhead, the ship rolled again and this time they heard, even above the wind and rain, a soft, reassuring splash. The next flash showed an empty railing below.

They turned and slid back toward the ship's entrance. Other deck chairs had blown against the railing, companions to Maggie's empty one. Every women fell at least once in the short distance to the entrance. Hadley grabbed the comforter from the corner and dived toward the door. The wind was blowing so hard she couldn't pull it open. Mary Rose grabbed the handle and together they pulled it open enough for Robbie to brace her leg inside the door and push while they pulled.

They literally fell inside.

The hall was empty. They stood and limping and dripping, made their way to the warmth of their stateroom.

## *I Remember, I Remember*

They stripped out of their wet clothes and draped them over Maggie's empty bed. They dried with the fluffy cruise line towels and clambered into pajamas and robes and warm slippers.

Hadley and Robbie stood over the bathtub and wrung out the comforter as best they could, crying along with the water dripping from it. When no more water came out, they draped it over a chair near the heater vent to dry.

As soon as she slipped into her house slippers, Robbie called their steward and asked for a pot of hot chocolate. "And if you have a candle, that would be very nice," she said.

"It's a good night for hot chocolate and a scented candle," the steward said. Robbie waited by the door until the tray of hot chocolate and candle arrived, opened the door just enough to take the tray and slip five dollars into the young man's hand.

"He didn't see anything," she said, motioning to the comforter and wet clothes draped all over the room.

# Gone is the Sailor

Hadley poured three cups of hot chocolate. Robbie lit the candle that was safe in a glass chimney – safety matches provided – and they stood around their little table in silence. Then Hadley raised her cup, "to Maggie," she said.

"To Maggie," the others replied.

"Oh, Maggie," Hadley began. "I will never forget you in those oversized black fatigues when we closed down the porno shop."

"Maggie," Robbie said. "When I was so scared in the hospital you were the first to hold my hand and the one to point out that I wasn't talking in quotes any more because I was more my own person now."

"Maggie," Mary Rose said, "my only regret is that we can't go to Africa to find your son now. But you'll be together someday," and she began to cry again.

They talked about Maggie and to Maggie for a very long time, and when they had finished, Robbie began softly:

Maggie, in the Spring,

When the first crocus pokes its head out of the ground

We think of you. And we remember.

We remember

In the Summer,

When the blazing heat wilts the rose petals

And paints unsightly cracks in the ground,

We think of you and we remember,

We remember.

In the Autumn,

When the trees are ablaze with color

And our shoes make crackling sounds as we walk

We think of you and we remember,

We remember.

And in the Winter

When we stand at our window to watch a blizzard

Whirl around our grief and loneliness,

We think of you and we remember,

We remember.

There was silence. The ship rocked. The rain diminished. The candle flickered gently and gave off a soft vanilla fragrance. Mary Rose leaned down and blew out the candle. "Goodbye good Maggie," she whispered. "Goodbye good friend and soul sister."

They sat together in silence that night. No one went to bed.

The comforter was nearly dry as they began docking procedures the next morning. Their clothes were nearly dry as well and packed away. Hadley lifted the comforter that had held Maggie as she died and spread it evenly across her bed. Only their sneakers had refused to dry, so Mary Rose put them in the shopping bag that had carried the rain jackets her casino winnings had purchased, bunched the colored tissue paper the clerk had added so she would appear to be carrying a simple, tasteful gift off the ship. "It's hard to see only three pairs of sneakers in here," she said as she packed. She began to cry again. Hadley and Robbie simply nodded, their eyes filling with tears as well.

The big ship shuddered to a stop and they pulled their suitcases out the door and into the hall.

Guests were laughing and chattering. Excitement filled the hallway, the elevator and the huge foyer leading to the landing ramps. As they walked out, nodding to the goodbyes and thank yous from the crew, Mary Rose noticed a young women concentrating on counting each passenger as they walked by. "They're going to be short one," she said.

"They'll go over the ship and think they miscounted," Hadley said and they walked down the ramp toward their

Hummer parked in the garage. The day was bright and sunny, a perfect day to come home from a cruise.

They took off their sun glasses as soon as they stepped into the garage elevator. They got off, along with five or six other people, on their level and walked toward the Hummer. As they got closer they saw a tall young man in navy blue pants and brown jacket leaning against the big vehicle. He had sandy hair, black running shoes and was wearing expensive sun glasses, even in the dark garage. His arms were folded and he looked impatient. When he spotted the three women he removed his glasses, stepped away from the Hummer and smiled.

"Any of you H. Margaret Patten?" he asked. They looked at each other.

"Dead meat now for sure," Robbie whispered.

Hadley stepped forward, "Maggie Patten started this cruise with us, but she's not with us now," she said. She smiled as if nothing at all out of the ordinary had happened and introduced Mary Rose and Robbie.

"I'm detective Joe Salvatore," the young man said. "do you know where I could find Hortence?"

"Hortence?" they said together.

Detective Salvatore pulled a small notebook out of his jacket pocket. "H. as in Hortence Margaret Patten," he said, and he looked at each of the women.

"We only knew her as Maggie," Hadley said.

"Who would name a baby 'Hortence'? Mary Rose said. Robbie did an eye roll and shrugged.

"You say she came on the cruise with you. Where is she now?" He's smarter than he looks, Robbie thought.

Hadley looked at the other two, "She went onto the island stop with us." She opened her purse, pulled out a ship schedule and handed it to Joe Salvatore. "We definitely saw her there."

"She was not in the dining room that same night when we got back to the ship," Robbie added.

"And she didn't show up this morning when we left the ship," Mary Rose said.

Detective Salvatore looked at three tired, innocent-looking faces and shook his head. "Have a fight?"

"Friends sometimes have disagreements," Hadley said, nodding her head. "There were a lot of shuttles going from that island to the mainland." She looked at Joe again and smiled.

"Well – that's about all I'm going to do on this case. If she surfaces let me know."

"I really doubt she'll surface," Hadley said.

"I'm not counting on it," Robbie said.

"Gone for good," Mary Rose added.

Officer Salvatore handed each one of them his card. Hadley looked at it.

"Homicide?"

"A lady named Millicent Millet claimed both her father Homer, and his sister Hortence, poisoned their spouses out in the Sand Hills of Nebraska. This is mainly a courtesy visit from our department for the sheriff out there."

"Poisoned?"

"Who knows? The old man died a few months ago. He had his wife cremated. We don't know if Hortence buried her husband's body or just put an urn in his grave in Omaha.

Personally, I think it's too much trouble to bother with. I have eighteen killings waiting for me back at the office. If they want to do more, let 'em." He smiled at the ladies, nodded and started to walk away.

"Detective Salvatore," Hadley said loudly. He turned and walked back toward them. "May I ask how you found us?"

"Easy. You have a state-of-the-art GPS in that Hummer. The police in Omaha tracked you from the time you left the Sand Hills until now. Seems some attorney in Omaha reported you missing, the retirement place said only one of your cars was gone, told him it was owned by Hortence. The attorney made a call to this Homer Millet and some Hispanic lady told him you'd been there and taken the Hummer and trailer. Once the attorney..." he flipped open his notebook, "David Winfield, found out you were all right he let it go."

"David," Hadley whispered. "Good boy, son."

Joe Salvatore pocketed his notebook, nodded again and walked away.

They loaded their suitcases into the Hummer and climbed in. Hadley drove, Robbie sat up front and Mary Rose sat alone in the back seat. They were quiet as Hadley wound out of the garage, through the city and onto the interstate leading to their campground. Then suddenly Mary Rose began to snicker. "Homer and Hortence," she said, "they both had really bad marriage karma," and she laughed louder.

Hadley joined in, then Robbie began to giggle. It felt good after all their tears.

"Wonder what they used to poison them? Robbie said.

"Are bull snakes poisonous?" Mary Rose asked, and they laughed and chatted all the way to the campground.

# Home

"She's at work with Polly," Hadley said. Since she was the tallest, she had stood on tip toe, peered into Polly's Airstream and not seen or heard Edith Ann. As she and Mary Rose hitched the trailer to the Hummer, Robbie wrote a note to put in Polly's mailbox. "Edith Ann has found a home with you. She loves you and so do we. Enjoy her and you two take care of each other," it was signed "The BOOB girls."

They gassed the Hummer at the truck stop, Hadley dashed into the bank in the truck stop for just a minute and they pulled onto the interstate without saying goodbye to Polly Panchero or Edith Ann.

Willy Nelson was singing *On the Road Again* from their CD player as they headed east toward Omaha, and after a short time, they were all three singing along. They had found the adventure of their lives together. Mary Rose had found a new, vibrant personality, Robbie had found her own poetry in her soul, Hadley had found a gentle new romance and Maggie had found the resting place she wanted.

Polly Panchero found sixty thousand dollars in a new savings account when she deposited her check at the truck stop bank. When she looked surprised, the teller had handed her an envelope. Inside was a note that read, "Study hard. Finish school. Be proud. The BOOB girls." Polly had taken the savings account book back to her truck, picked up Edith Ann and cried into her soft fur while the little dog licked her tears away.

# Epilogue

Meadow Lakes Retirement Community was decked out for
the holidays. They had been gone nine months, a proper time
for new birthings. They were going to celebrate Christmas
day in Hadley's spacious apartment. Mary Rose's daughters
were all coming, along with their husbands and children.
Since Robbie had only distant cousins spread all across the
country, she invited Wiley Vondra to be her guest because
he had only distant cousins spread all across the country.
Hadley's son David and two of her college-aged grandchildren
would be there. The skinny  third wife was spending the
holidays at a fat farm in Phoenix with her obese sister. Most
importantly, Wes Longbow was coming. Since he was already
past retirement age, he and Hadley had talked for hours on
the phone and through emails about his coming to Omaha
and starting a private detective agency where he could putter
around part time. They were working on an appropriate
Indian name for it. "Kemosabe and Kemosabe" was Hadley's
favorite since she planned to work with him, but Wes didn't
really seem to be a Lone Ranger type.

They were seated at table 12 at lunch time, planning
the Christmas menu, which would include macaroni and
cheese, Maggie's favorite, when Robbie whispered, "Look!"
and pointed to the other side of the dining room.

Walking amongst the tables, looking for a place to sit
in the crowded room, was a mousey, dowdy woman. Her
gray hair was pulled into a tight bun at the nape of her neck,

ugly dark-rimmed glasses had slipped down on her nose. She wore a plain cotton dress and blue sweater. Her shoes were a plain ugly brown and she wore white anklets. Robbie noticed that her slip hung down in the back about two inches below her dress. She spotted the empty chair at table 12, hesitated, looked around again and moved awkwardly toward them. She put a large, shapeless purse down on the floor. "Hello," she said quietly. "My name is Patricia Whack. May I join you? This seems to be the only open chair."

Mary Rose stood up. She was wearing a lavender wool pantsuit. A bright red scarf was around her neck and draped over one shoulder. It matched her red nails and red shoes. Her hair was the usual masterpiece by Peyton Clairborne. She held out her hand across the table and the homely little lady put her own limp hand in Mary Rose's. "Sit down, Patty Whack. Make yourself at home," She released the small hand, motioned for the woman to sit down, then spread one arm toward Hadley and the other toward Robbie. "We're the BOOB girls."

Visit the girls and Joy Johnson at:

**www.theboobgirls.com**

**The BOOB Girls** are available on Kindle and Nook.

Joy is an international speaker who has presented delightful *Boob Girl* programs across the country.

Ask her about speaking at your group. You can email Joy at joy.johnson@msn.com

**Other grief resources available through**

**www.centering.org**

# About the Author

Joy Johnson is over 75 now. With her late husband, Dr. Marvin Johnson, she founded Centering Corporation, North America's oldest and largest bereavement resource center, and Ted E. Bear Hollow, Omaha area's center for grieving children. Joy has written or edited over 100 books on grief, many for children. After she retired in 2009, she began writing **The BOOB Girls**: The Burned Out Old Broads at Table 12, a comedy-mystery series for senior women.

Joy has three children and six grandchildren. She lives in Omaha, Nebraska, with her husband, Ted Brown and a tabby cat named Margaret Thatcher. Like her characters, she is a funny, active beautiful BOOB Girl.

# If you enjoy this book, you'll love and laugh with:

*The Boob Girls:*
*The Burned Out Broads at Table 12*

*The Boob Girls II:*
*Lies, Spies and Cinnamon Roles*

*The Boob Girls III:*
*Sandhills and Shadows*

*The Boob Girls IV:*
*Murder at Meadow Lakes*

*The Boob Girls V:*
*The Secret of the Red Cane*

*The Boob Girls VI:*
*From the Eye of the Moose*

*The Boob Girls VII:*
*Ten Little Puritans*

*The Boob Girls VIII:*
*Learning to Love Willie*

**www.theboobgirls.com**